Mr Roberts' House

Catherine Blackmore

First published 2021
by Rowanvale Books Ltd
The Gate
Keppoch Street
Roath
Cardiff
CF24 3JW
www.rowanvalebooks.com

A CIP catalogue record for this book is available from the British Library.

Paperback ISBN: 978-1-912655-94-6

This book is dedicated to Nunc, who adored his vegetable garden. You are dearly loved and missed but never forgotten xx

To my husband, Steve. A big thank you for all the love and support you have shown me while I wrote this book.

To my parents, for their encouragement.

Karen, thank you once again for all your help.

Freedom, thank you for your advice on some of the chapters.

Shannon, a big thank you for all the advice and reading you did on this book. I could not have done it without you.

To my sister Liz, who was the inspiration for the character Lou.

Contents

Prologue

Rain lashes against the window. Staring through the glass at the blurry hillside, Mr Roberts pauses for a moment. Placing his hands against his lower back, he approaches the male servant.

'You must be very highly regarded by my friend?' Mr Roberts says.

The servant continues to dust the sideboard. 'I would like to think so, sir,' he replies.

A smirk creeps across Mr Roberts' face. Stepping closer, he waves an empty tumbler at the servant. The servant picks up the decanter from the sideboard and pours Mr Roberts a brandy.

Leaning forward, Mr Roberts raises his volume. 'I have recently moved into a new house with a new wife and I need a good servant. Would you be interested?'

Refilling the glass with brandy once more, the servant makes eye contact with Mr Roberts. 'I appreciate the offer, sir, but I have a good position here,' he answers, wiping the decanter down before placing it back on the sideboard.

'However, I am offering a better position with attractive wages. Think about it, and stop by the house tomorrow afternoon to discuss the matter further,' Mr Roberts insists.

***

The servant glances at the address on the notepaper Mr Roberts had given him, and as he looks up, the sign with the street name comes into view. He turns into the street and strolls down the cobbled avenue to number 13. A young maid opens the door. She curtsies with a smile and steps aside to let him through.

'This way, sir,' she whispers.

The maid shows him to the living room and, turning on her heel, dashes from the room. Moments later, Mr Roberts enters, heading for the drinks cabinet.

'Have you thought about the offer?' he asks.

Raising his eyebrow, the servant steps back. Glancing at Mr Roberts, he asks, 'I have, sir. Although, I have a few questions. What position would I hold here? And also, would this be a live-in?'

Mr Roberts pours a whiskey and nods to the man. 'Would you like one?'

'Yes, sir.'

As Mr Roberts hands him the glass, he answers the questions. 'I'm in need of a butler. The young girl who answered the door—oh, what's her name… Mary— needs a firm hand, as she can be a bit lazy. Then there is the garden, and so on. I am a busy man and have no time to deal with such issues, and my wife… well, let's just say she doesn't have a brain, so she can't deal with such issues. This is where you come in. I need you to control the staff.'

The servant's eyes widen; he takes a step back as he shakes his head. 'A butler!'

'Yes. My friend has spoken very highly of you and the work you have done. I spoke to him this morning and he is willing to let you come and work here, if you would like the position. It is also live-in.'

The doorbell rings. A few moments later, a woman walks into the room. Placing the bags on a chair, she starts to babble. 'Henry, I bought another dress,' she says as she removes her hat and gloves. 'A man will stop by later with the food, as I had no more hands to carry it.' Wandering over to Mr Roberts, she kisses his cheek.

'Ada, what have I said about showing affection in front of others?' he scolds, darting his eyes at her.

'I'm sorry, Henry; I didn't know you had company,' she whispers, diverting her eyes to the floor. Her hand trembles as she twists the diamond and sapphire ring on her finger. Lifting her head, she meets her husband's gaze.

'This man may be our new servant. He was just about to give his answer,' Henry adds.

Ada's eyes glisten when she looks at the servant. Her lips curl into a smile as he nods at her, returning the gesture.

Turning to Mr Roberts, he says, 'I will take the job. When would you like me to start?'

Mr Roberts smiles at the man and rings the servants' bell, hoping the maid will respond quickly. 'What is your name? My friend did mention it, but it escapes me at the moment.'

'Richard Harris, sir.'

A grin creeps across Mr Roberts' face. Gripping Richard's hand, they shake on the deal.

'Welcome to the Roberts' house, Mr Harris.'

Chapter 1

In the darkness, a poltergeist moves through the bedroom and seethes at the latest owner of the house. It glances down at the side table; a pipe is leaning against an ashtray as a smoky scent hangs in the air. The old man is asleep, oblivious to the poltergeist's presence. Baring its teeth, it creeps towards him. Bending down, closing the gap between them, it grins.

'Soon, you'll be where I am. Enjoy it while you can,' it whispers.

The man stirs and opens his eyes. He scans his room and spots nothing. He must have dreamt of hearing someone speak. As he drifts back to sleep, the poltergeist comes closer and whispers in his ear.

'I can't wait for the children to arrive—they are so much fun to tease. It's up to you, old man!' it mocks.

An eerie stillness fills the house as the man sleeps. The poltergeist paces and yells. Nothing. It picks up a book from the side table and throws it across the room. The man jolts upright. A smile creeps across its face.

Again, the man stares into the darkness and sees nothing. He tries to settle back down, but memories surface from a previous night. Something brushes against his arm. He pulls his arm away as sweat trickles from his forehead. *What do these nightmares mean?* In a nauseating rush, the details of his dreams return to him.

Standing by the window, the poltergeist smiles. 'These are real nightmares. Someone is haunting you. I'm doing this. My message is simple: I want you out of my home, as you have no right to be here. I know you can hear me. Ignoring me won't work,' it says as it leaves the room. 'I'll have fun with the children instead.'

The man's eyes dart to the door. His heart pounds as a breeze brushes across his face. Glancing at the open window, he puts the incident down to the wind.

Wide awake, he pulls the covers off and heads downstairs. He enters the kitchen. Picking up the kettle, he takes the lid off and fills it with water. He plugs the kettle back in and clicks the button. A creak on the stairs makes him jump.

Trembling, he needs something stronger. He heads to the living room, next to the kitchen. He opens the liquor cabinet and pours a shot of whiskey, knocking it back. Tremors rush through his body as he holds the glass. It shakes in his hand. His left hand steadies his right as he sets the tumbler down. Pouring another large whiskey, he knocks it back also. The steps get closer.

Freezing, he focuses on the wall in front of him. Chills race through his body as sweat drips from his forehead. Turning around, there is nothing in the darkness. Relief washes over him. He turns back to the cabinet and sets the glass down.

As he leaves the room, there's a shattering of glass. His nerves shatter with it. He turns the light on; shards of a broken tumbler glint on the floor. His eyes widen, his mouth opens, the hairs rise on the back of his neck. Scratching his head, he edges back towards the cabinet. Touching the base of his neck, he frowns and bends down, picking up the shards of glass from the carpet, while the poltergeist laughs.

'I'm letting you know I'm here and I won't be ignored,' it scorns.

The man heads back to his room as the poltergeist follows behind him. As he settles down in bed, an icy touch strokes his face. Panic grips him. He doesn't have time to dwell on nightmares; the girls are coming tomorrow.

Chapter 2

In the warmth of this beautiful day, I can't wait to get there. I run as fast as I can, passing every beautiful house, while my sister lags behind me. Streaks of light peer through the tall trees. As the leaves sway in the breeze, a shadow catches my eye. Glancing over my shoulder, nothing is there, but I see that my sister is gaining on me. I still get to the front gate first.

At the top of the stairs stands a giant red door with a heavy and prominent brass doorknob. I stare for a moment, tugging at my earlobe, taking a step back as my body goes numb. Glancing to my right, there are stairs going down to another door with a large bay window next to it, but it looks unloved and lonely. *Maybe the ghost still lives there?*

The red door opens and there stands my uncle with a smile on his face, his arms open wide, ready to give us both hugs and kisses. Taking a deep breath, I run into his arms along with my sister, who has finally caught up.

'How are my girls today?' he asks with a smile.

'I'm fine. Can't wait to go in the garden,' I answer.

Tapping her foot while folding her arms, my sister asks, 'Do you have any ice cream?'

'After dinner. Now go inside.'

We enter the long hall; it is big and bright with light yellow walls, a high ceiling and old Victorian tiles on the floor. A laundry room is in front of us; turning right, there is a huge staircase on the left-hand side. In between the laundry room and staircase is a short corridor, and straight in front, there is a door with a stained-glass window, leading to an enormous garden. Next to the door is a small staircase going down to the basement. The entrance to the right leads to a living room, and straight ahead is the kitchen.

We sprint to the living room, dump our coats and head towards the back door, almost knocking our mum over, who came in the front door behind us.

'No running in the house!' she shouts after us.

Ignoring her, we run down the wooden stairs. As my foot touches the third step, it creaks. When my sister places her foot on the same step, nothing. We test the stairs again, running back down them, but I get to the last step without a creak. However, when Lou steps on the second step, it creaks.

'Why are the stairs making weird sounds in different places?' Lou asks as the colour drains from her face.

'You worry too much, Lou,' I insist, although we both know it's strange.

'Do you want to get the bogey out of the shed?'

'I'll race you,' I answer.

As we approach the shed, the sun disappears and a darkness surrounds it. The warmth of the day is replaced by a chill. When I exhale, a cloud of condensation escapes. We both place a hand on the shed's rusty door handle. A burning sensation shoots through us and we remove our hands. *I hope the ghost isn't on the other side!*

Covering my hand with my T-shirt, I pull on the rusty handle. At first, I can't make out anything inside, but when the sun shines through the trees, the shed lights up. Reflecting the sun, the wheels glisten as the pram-based bogey reveals itself. Lou and I start tugging at the bogey—our go-kart—and eventually pull it free. *Yay, no ghost.*

For the next hour or so, we happily push each other around the garden, using the ropes to change direction.

When it is my turn to push, I glance up to one of the windows and a curtain moves.

'Lou, did you see that?' I ask.

She shrugs her shoulders without uttering a word. I glance through the kitchen window, and my uncle and mother are watching us play. They wave and I do the same.

A short time later, we are called in to have some food. When we get to the kitchen, Lou barges past me to sit next to our uncle.

'Can I go to the toilet before food?' I ask.

'Just be quick,' Mum tells me.

I get to the staircase and take a deep breath. I tiptoe up, but when my foot hits the fourth step, my body stiffens, refusing to allow me beyond this point. As I try to move my foot off the fourth step, it won't budge, so I turn on the spot and rush down the stairs back to the kitchen.

'That was quick!' Mum remarks, flicking her brown hair.

'I'll wait till after dinner,' I answer, not wanting to give the real reason.

'Ann, food can wait. Go and use the toilet,' Mum insists.

'I can't go. I have a feeling once I get to the fourth step.'

Mum glances at Uncle Art.

'Do as your mum has asked before dinner gets cold,' he interjects.

My uncle is tall and slim, with a slight belly and pure white hair. Sometimes he wears trousers with braces, depending on his mood. His passion is his garden, as he grows a variety of vegetables and fruit.

My sister volunteers to come with me, and we skip as we head to the stairs.

'I don't like going to the toilet on my own,' Lou voices as we tiptoe up the stairs.

'So it's not just me?'

'No. Last time we came here, I ran down the stairs so fast I almost fell.'

She sits on the edge of the bath as I use the toilet. When I'm finished, we head out of the bathroom. On the right is another set of stairs, which take you to the attic. We glance towards it. A cold breeze brushes past me, and as I hold Lou's hand, it is shaking and clammy. My heart races as we share a worried glance. *He must be up there, waiting.* No words escape our lips, and we rush downstairs. When I reach the table, I'm sweating.

'Ann, are you alright?' my uncle asks.

'I hate going to the bathroom upstairs. It's scary,' I answer.

'Louise, do you feel the same way as your sister?'

She nods in agreement as she shovels food into her mouth. My uncle glances at my mother.

'Everyone who comes to this house seems to think it is haunted,' he tells us. 'Your aunt swore there was something here, but I have never heard or seen anything.'

'I hate going to the bathroom as well,' Mum adds.

We soon change the subject and finish our food. My sister and I run to the living room so we can watch telly.

Entering the large living room, with its striped grey wallpaper with the odd flower on it, a sense of gloom and dominance paralyses me. Straight in front of me is a big bay window letting in a lot of light, with a red sofa sitting snugly under the windowsill and curtains to match draped either side. On the right is a dinner table with a large oval mirror encased in gold trim above it. The left part of the room is intimate, with a small telly in the corner on the same side as the sofa. There are two chairs in front of an electric fire.

After a few minutes there is a bang on the ceiling. We both jump.

'Did you hear that?' I shout.

Lou continues to watch telly, ignoring my question. Turning back to the telly, I carry on watching the program with Lou when it happens again.

We edge up the stairs, holding each other's hand. It seems to takes forever, but when we get to the top, we glance both ways. Nothing. Straight ahead is the bedroom that once belonged to my aunt. It's been a few years, and we all still miss her.

Lou and I stare at each other as we tiptoe forward. A thud from inside the room vibrates into the hallway. Drips of sweat trickle down my sister's face. Her bobbed brown hair is out of place; she's shaking uncontrollably. Tremors shoot through my body.

'Do you want to go back downstairs?' I ask her.

'I want to, but I want to know what the noise is,' she whispers.

My stomach churns as I slowly reach for the handle of my aunt's room. I pause for a moment before trying to turn it.

Clearing her throat, Lou mutters, 'I'll open the door, if you won't.'

We swap places and she tries to open the door.

'It's not easy, is it?' I state.

'Shut up!' Lou snaps back. 'Maybe if we try together, it would help.'

As we enter the room, everything is still in its place, the way my aunt left it before she died. The two big windows brighten up the room beautifully, only broken up by her dressing table. We look around, not touching anything. Believing our imaginations were playing tricks on us, we head towards the door. It slams shut.

I pull on the handle but it won't budge. Lou tries— nothing. We both yank on the handle, and still nothing. I detect a click as if the door is being locked. Panic now sets in. A laugh echoes around the room. Our eyes widen with fear; we pound on the door, screaming for help. I try the door again while Lou keeps beating her fists against it. We fall backwards as it opens. Looking at each other, without saying a word, we get to our feet and sprint from the room. The cackling laugh follows us down the stairs, but when we pass the fourth step from the bottom, it stops. Gasping for breath, I turn around and place my foot back on the fourth step. The laughing resumes. Then silence, until a voice says, 'Until next time, Ann.'

Chills rush through my body as the colour drains from my face. I dart back downstairs. Lou stares at me, touching her face.

'What happened?' she asks.

'When I put my foot on the fourth step, the laugh started again. Then the voice said, "until next time, Ann." I'm scared, Lou.'

'Do you think it's a g-ghost?' she stutters.

'I don't know,' I snap back.

'There you are! Looks like you have been running.' We both jump when we see Mum standing in front of us.

'You scared me!' Lou exclaims.

'Sorry. Dad called and he's been delayed, so we'll be staying the night,' Mum announces.

She disappears back into the kitchen. The glare we share with each other says it all. We make our way back to the living room and return to watching telly. A short time later, Mum and our uncle join us. We watch different programmes until it is time for bed.

The door to my aunt's room opens unaided, but Mum doesn't notice and just walks inside.

'We're staying in here tonight,' Mum tells us.

'Ann, you can have your own bed and I'll sleep with Mum,' Lou tells me.

'No, Lou—I think you should have a bed to yourself,' I spit back.

'No, you!' Lou shouts.

'No, you,' I insist.

'Stop the bickering, both of you,' Mum interjects.

We stop and stare at her, not saying a word.

'I love you both, but I think Ann being the eldest should have a bed all to herself,' Mum smiles at us.

My sister struts towards the bed with Mum and a smirk creeps across Lou's face as if she's won a competition. I hope when the morning comes, I'm still alive.

Chapter 3

I lie there wide awake with my head under the covers, waiting for something to happen. I peep out for a moment, observing my mum and sister, who are fast asleep. A creak comes from outside the bedroom door and I bury myself under the covers again. When the door closes, I exhale, thinking it must have been my uncle going to his room. Now relaxed, I drift off to sleep.

Something scrapes loudly across a table and my body starts shaking. I remove the covers. Something moves on my aunt's dressing table—a handheld mirror. Panic grips me as the mirror floats through the air towards me. I try to scream, but no words escape my lips. I'm paralysed by fear as the mirror gets closer. It gets to the side of the bed, only inches from my face, and tips forward as if it is bowing at me. Then the poltergeist shouts out.

'BOO!'

I try and scream again, but nothing comes out. I throw the covers over my head. My body trembles as I start to hyperventilate. The same eerie laugh as earlier makes me flinch as I clutch my nightdress. Now, it fades into the distance. Desperate to escape, I bolt out of bed and run, stumbling into the hallway in total darkness. I circle the same spot in the hope that light will peer through the dark, but there isn't any. I move sideways and touch a wall, searching for a light switch, but I don't find one. The bedroom door is still open, but

I can't detect the doorway. I edge away from the wall when someone speaks.

'Watch where you walk,' the voice snaps.

My lip trembles as I flinch. Rooted to the spot, I stutter, 'He—hello?'

'I said, "Watch where you're walking,"' the voice repeats.

'Who are you?' I ask, not wanting to have the answer. I am met with silence.

I repeat the question, raising my voice but there is no response. I sense something on my back, pushing me forward. I stretch my arms out to stop the force behind me, but it is too strong. Keeping my arms out, I make out the bedroom door, and the shoving stops. I listen to my sister snore and follow the sound. Finally, I find my bed. I jump in, duck under the covers and close my eyes tight.

In the morning, I sense a shaking motion, and when I open my eyes, my sister is there waking me up.

'Time to get up, Ann,' Lou insists.

'I've had a terrible night's sleep.'

'You have to get up, or you'll be on your own up here.'

I jump up and look at Lou. I glance at the dressing table—everything is back in its place.

'Something strange happened last night,' I say, turning back to Lou.

'Like what?' she asks.

I'm about to answer when, out the corner of my eye, I glimpse the hand mirror rising from the dressing table, moving left to right as if waving at me. I tug my sister's arm and point towards the mirror. When Lou turns to look, the mirror gestures in a bowing motion again. As the colour drains from her face, she steps backwards.

'Ann, do you see the mirror moving?' she whispers.

'This is what happened last night.'

The mirror makes its way towards us, and when it stops, it is in front of my sister. Lou tries to grab it, but it jumps out of the way. Once again, it hovers in front of her. Lou edges her arm forward and reaches for the mirror. When she falls down, I rush over to help.

'Don't touch the mirror!' the poltergeist yells.

We run for the doorway but can't go through. The door is open, but something is stopping us.

'Let us through!' I demand.

'No,' the poltergeist snaps.

'What do you want?' I cry.

Lou grabs my hand and squeezes it, almost crushing my fingers. She starts to whimper.

'Soon, but not yet,' the poltergeist replies.

'That's not an answer. Now let us out!' I yell.

'Too many questions. Bye.'

An eerie silence falls across the room for a moment, only to be broken by Lou's piercing scream.

'What is it?' I shout over the scream.

Lou stops, glancing at me with her bulging eyes.

'Didn't you hear that?' she cries.

'Hear what?' I ask, my eyes darting around the room.

'The voice was in my ear and it shouted "boo!",' she blubbers, tears streaming down her face.

Heading for the open doorway, we sprint into the hallway. Lou darts down the stairs, but when I try to follow, something stops me. I try again, but a force keeps stopping me from stepping onto the staircase. My pulse starts racing and my head becomes lighter as I stumble backwards. I turn towards the bedroom but my body is stiff. Swivelling on the spot, I head for the bathroom, but again I can't move.

Glancing at my uncle's room, I try and put my foot forward, but the force is stopping me. I turn, but realise I'm facing the attic stairs again. The force pushes me towards them; I try to pull away but my body is stiff.

Then the force pushes me up. With each step, my pleas go unnoticed. Tears stream down my face and, as I get closer, my body shivers. Turning the corner on the stairs, there are two doors. One starts to open. I try to turn around, but I am being forced forward.

'I don't want to be up here!' I scream.

When the room comes into view, I struggle to get free, but the force is too strong.

'Let me go!' I cry.

This room once held my aunt's sewing collection, but it is all gone. When I reach the doorway, my eyes dart around the room, but all that's inside is a single chair.

Chapter 4

My knees lock as my body stiffens. I start to wriggle free, but the force regains control. It pushes me forward and forces me onto the chair. I shake uncontrollably as I try and move, but I can't; it's as if I'm tied to the chair. The lights fade away into darkness. An eerie laugh echoes around the room. Tears run down my face as my stomach tenses.

'Let me go!' I beg.

'I'm having too much fun,' the poltergeist teases.

'I can't see you,' I cry as the tears run down my face and onto my lap.

'It isn't time yet,' the poltergeist replies.

'What do you want?' I ask, my eyes darting around the room.

'To play!' the poltergeist exclaims.

'I'm frightened, and I want to go,' I plead.

There is no reply. As I continue to shake, something cold passes through my body. I open my mouth, but no sound leaves my lips. The laughter starts again, and then silence. I try to wriggle free but I'm stuck.

After a few minutes, I'm in a different room. A man and a woman appear in front of me, but they are dressed strangely. The clothes look old fashioned. A scent of flowers mixed with a musty odour hangs in the air. The woman crosses her arms as she lifts her head. The man shakes his finger at her, his teeth bared. Then he raises his hand and strikes her across the cheek. Tears trickle down her face as she lifts her hand to touch where he hit. I close my eyes, only opening them again a few minutes later when I hear the couple move away. When I do, the woman is falling from the window. Her screams vibrate around the room. My stomach churns. As her body hits the ground, a thud echoes in my ears.

I struggle once more but it's no good. A few minutes pass, and another man gets up on a table. There is a noose hanging from the ceiling; he puts it around his neck, then waits for a moment, glancing towards the door. I follow his eyes but no one is there. When I turn back, the table has been knocked over and the man's lifeless body is swaying in the air. I open my mouth and a scream escapes my lips.

What is this? Do I really want the answer?

Now, back in the attic, the room fills with rays of sunlight. I try again to wriggle free and this time I can move. I jump up and the chair falls over. As I dart for the door, it slams shut. I grab the handle and pull with all the strength I have. It opens.

When I dash through the doorway, the poltergeist screams, 'You can't leave!'

I ignore the voice and keep running down the stairs. I almost slip as I turn into the spiral of the staircase. Mum is waiting at the bottom with her arms crossed and eyebrows drawn together.

'Where were you?' she asks.

'I was in the attic,' I say, trying to catch my breath.

Mum narrows her eyes and she shouts, 'You shouldn't be up there!'

'I didn't want to be up there, but I was forced,' I stutter. 'A ghost took me to the attic.'

Mum raises an eyebrow. 'I know we mentioned the house might be haunted, but no one has ever seen anything. I think you're letting your imagination run away with you.'

'I'm not!' I yell back.

'Enough, Ann. Now, you'd better eat your breakfast before your dad gets here,' she insists.

Standing my ground, I cross my arms and widen my stance. 'I'm telling the truth,' I grumble.

Mum widens her eyes and folds her arms while tapping her foot.

Letting out a huff, I stomp my way into the kitchen. *Could it be an overactive imagination?*

As I'm finishing my breakfast, Uncle Art comes into the kitchen.

'Your sister is in the garden, if you want to go out there with her,' he says as I put my bowl in the sink.

'Has she got the bogey out?' I giggle.

'Yes, she has, but she's pushing it around at the moment, so go and have fun with her,' he laughs as he starts washing the dishes.

Glancing up the stairs, a shiver goes through me. I shake my head and sprint out into the garden. Lou and I play for a while with the bogey before we're called inside. Walking back up the wooden stairs, I glance up to the attic window, but nothing is there. Edging to the end of the balcony, I peer over the side into the small courtyard, but there is only the concrete yard below. I stare for a few moments. My mum calls my name once more.

When I pass the basement stairs, a whisper comes close to my ear. 'Until next time, Ann!'

Dashing over to Mum, I take my bag and coat from her.

'Your dad is waiting in the car, so it's time to go,' she says.

Uncle Art appears from behind her with a broad grin across his face. Opening his arms wide, he says, 'Let's have a big hug before you go.'

I run into his arms and hug him tight.

'See you soon, Ann.'

I gaze up at him and he kisses me on the cheek.

'Don't forget these,' he adds. In his hand are a couple of bars of chocolate. 'One is for you and the other is for Lou.'

I nod, a smile creeping across my face as I take the chocolate. 'Thank you, Uncle Art,' I beam, and run in case he changes his mind.

Chapter 5

The ghost stares at Art pottering in the garden from the large kitchen window. As he turns, he lets out a huff, knocking over a bottle on the counter. This room once had a glittering glass chandelier in the centre of the ceiling as a feature piece, and underneath it a mahogany table which would sit ten comfortably. There had been a sideboard in the corner with decanters that held many spirits. The only original feature left is the window.

Storming out of the kitchen, the ghost enters the living room. He sits in Art's chair by the fire and sighs, a grin creeping across his face. However, when he gazes at the fireplace, the smile disappears. Clenching his fist, the ghost punches the armrest. Memories after his death, the ghost can recall, such as an eye-catching mahogany fireplace. Many parties had taken place in this home. Every guest would comment on the beautiful mantel with its roaring fire and the mirror that sat above the full width of the hearth. Those were the days—people took risks and achieved greatness. Today, people didn't do such things. Years later, it was replaced by an electric fire.

And yet, any memories of his life before death escape him. He glides towards the mirror to see the reflection of the man he once was, but there's nothing. Even his name eludes him. Condemned to this eternity is worse than living. Everything has changed.

Papers are scattered all over the thick mahogany table, so he gathers them up into a neat pile. Stepping back, he stares at the pile. *Why did I do that?*

The back door opens and the ghost retreats upstairs. He enters the room that once belonged to Art's wife. Passing through the two single beds, he stops at the wardrobe. Pulling on the handle, it clicks and swings open. Peering inside, he rifles through the items, searching for any reference to the past. The stairs creak with each of Art's footsteps; the ghost stops his search and follows Art into his bathroom.

He picks up Art's toothbrush and holds it in front of him, but there is no reaction. Art turns on the tap and places the plug in the bath. Picking up the towel, Art dries his hands. A bar of soap just misses his face. The ghost lunges towards Art but falls through.

He stomps out of the bathroom, muttering to himself. 'This isn't over, Art!'

A short time later, Art wanders into his room and gets ready for bed. Out of instinct Art heads to the sink but remembers he needs to fix it, which is why he used the main sink. The ghost taps his foot, folding his arms. He starts pacing and knocks Art's clothes off the chair. He grins as Art picks them up and places them back. As Art's eyes grow heavy, the ghost moves the curtains. One brushes against the sink, then slides back into place. Art's eyes widen as he jolts upright.

'Now we are getting somewhere,' the ghost says, a smirk creeping across his face.

Art clicks the button on the lamp, but the light doesn't come on. Removing the covers, he plods across the room to switch on the main light, but he stumbles to the ground. The ghost bellows at Art's misfortune. Art staggers back to his feet as the ghost brushes past him. Art's body trembles. When the ghost passes the window, the light hides him, but when he steps into the darkness, his outline is visible. Art doesn't notice him.

The ghost storms out, slamming the door behind him. Art jumps.

'Who's there?' he shouts.

Nothing but silence fills the room. Art shakes his head and wanders back to bed.

'I know you want to believe it's only you in this house,' the ghost says in a sharp tone as he re-enters the bedroom.

Art freezes for a few moments. The ghost glares at him.

'You can hear me, so talk to me,' the ghost demands.

Art ignores him.

'I SAID TALK TO ME!'

Again, Art doesn't reply. The ghost grabs the chair and throws it across the room. The clothes scatter all over the room. He flings the wardrobe doors open and tosses the clothes and shoes behind him. Still seething, he storms into the next room. He knocks the contents of the dressing table to the floor. Grabbing the drawer handles, he pulls them out and flings the drawers across the room. Letting out a huff, he turns around and pushes the bed into the wall.

Art storms into his wife's room for the first time in years. 'You have an issue with me, fine! But do not disrespect my late wife!' he seethes.

His wife was meticulous about her possessions and her home. If he entered the hallway with his boots on, she would yell at him to go outside and remove them, always saying she had just cleaned the floor. After she died, whenever he entered the hallway with his boots on, only coldness and silence greeted him. The realisation she had passed away would hit him hard.

The ghost stops and turns towards Art. 'Why do you ignore me?'

'I wasn't sure until tonight. My wife told me the house was haunted, but I didn't believe her. Now tidy my wife's things and leave me alone,' Art demands.

'We need to talk,' the ghost pleads.

'I have nothing to say to you. Now leave me alone,' Art repeats.

Art walks back to his bedroom. A man's body hangs in the doorway. Art steps back, trembling as he stares at the swaying body.

'Nice parlour trick. Now leave me alone,' he hisses, but there is no response.

Leaving the room, the ghost wanders the house, continuing his search for anything to remind him of his past. Entering the kitchen, he looks out over the large garden, kicking the wall below the window. He needs Art's help as there are many questions he needs answered.

Thundering footsteps get closer. The ghost turns and sees a shadowy male figure in front of him. The room turns bloody red and a putrid odour fills the air as the figure charges at him.

'This is your fault!' the poltergeist screams.

The ghost falls through the glass window, the poltergeist holding onto him.

The ghost has never seen another like the poltergeist in all the years he has occupied the house. He can't understand what is happening. They land in the courtyard below. The ghost is lying on the floor as the poltergeist passes through him, sucked into the concrete by something. The poltergeist's terrifying scream lingers but gets quieter until it finally disappears.

Scratching his head, the ghost stays there for a few moments.

Chapter 6

Curled up on Uncle Art's armchair, I'm glued to a programme on the telly. Uncle Art is in the kitchen preparing dinner.

'Hello, Ann. Remember me?' the poltergeist says.

'Go away!' I screech, my body shaking.

'Where is your sister?' the poltergeist asks.

'Go away,' I beg.

I need the bathroom, but Lou isn't here and I can't ask my uncle to go with me. I wriggle in the chair, trying to hold on, but the need grows. Running to the stairs, I glance up. I breathe in and out as I edge up them. Crossing the fourth step, fear grips me. My heart palpitates with each step upwards. I close my eyes for a moment and, as I reach the last step, I hold my breath. Exhaling, I move towards the bathroom. Leaving the door open wide, I hover over the toilet. The door opposite is open; the room holds only a sink. A man is standing there. He smiles, and I return the gesture. He disappears, and I scream as fear takes over.

OMG, the ghost is real!

I start to run but he reappears again and grabs my hand. He drags me to the attic, but this time it looks different. There is a bed, a side table and a wardrobe.

'What is this?' the ghost demands.

'I don't know. I've never seen this before,' I cry as the tears stream down my cheeks. I wipe the tears with my arm. My eyes widen as I stare at him.

'Why are you crying?' the ghost yells.

'You keep bringing me here, and it's scary,' I sob.

'Um, I have never brought you here before,' the ghost says, scratching his forehead.

I run towards the door but something catches my eye—a photograph. Thinking I've escaped, the ghost is throwing things around the room. I tiptoe past him and grab the photograph, hiding it under my T-shirt as I dart for the door. Once downstairs, I find my uncle, and take a deep breath.

'Uncle Art, did you have a bedroom up in the attic?'

'What have you been told about going in the attic?' he says. I gaze at the floor and brush my hand through my hair. 'Ann, there are two rooms up in the attic. So, at some point in time, they were bedrooms. I'm guessing… servants' quarters. Now, one is empty as it was once your aunt's sewing room. The other is full of different things.' Pausing for a moment, he adds, 'Ann, come with me.'

He takes me to the basement. The first room we come to on the left is a kitchen. It hasn't been used in a long time and is cluttered with chairs and carpets, but a small area is open. Old, pale blue cupboards with wooden handles stand out, but they are covered in a thick layer of dust. In the middle of the room is a wooden table, and against the wall opposite the window are household items like a single bed and more rolls of carpet. The window is covered in dirt, so the light can't get in. Opposite the kitchen is a slatted door. When I pull on it, dust particles float in the air. I start coughing as the dust travels into my mouth and up my nose. Peering through, a stale smell hits me, so I slam it shut.

'I see you found the toilet,' my uncle laughs.

'It's dirty!' I say, holding my nose, though it doesn't smell anymore.

My uncle points upwards, and above the door is a row of golden bells.

'This area was for servants. A kitchen, the toilet, and through there is the living area.'

Glancing through the living room door, I notice a front door on the other side of the room. Turning to Uncle Art, I ask, 'Does that door lead to the street?'

'Yes. Servants were not allowed to use the main door, and if you follow this hall, you'll see a back door.'

'This one leads to the little courtyard?' I ask.

He opens the back door and I step outside. The courtyard isn't big. The kitchen window is on the right, and at the end of the yard on the left are some stairs leading to the garden.

'Can I go up the stairs?' I ask.

'Go on then, and I'll meet you at the basement entrance.'

I run up the stairs and open the gate, skipping towards the main steps in the garden. A sense of dread sweeps over me. My body shivers with each step, but it's a scorching day. I run across the balcony, and my knees buckle beneath me.

'Clumsy girl,' the poltergeist says.

My uncle comes over to me and holds me.

'Ann, are you alright?' he asks.

'Yes, I'm okay.'

I walk inside with my uncle, but it's dark. I call out to him, but there's no response. I'm all alone. I startle as a cold hand grabs mine.

Chapter 7

A sliver of light appears as the icy hand drags me down a pathway. Silence fills the air, and the deeper I go down this pathway, the darker it becomes. I try to yank my hand free, but the grip gets tighter, sending shivers through me. Now, whispers come from all directions. A pungent smell of rotting flesh travels up my nose, turning my stomach. Further down the path, unpleasant moans and whimpers of pain linger in the air. My lip quivers and tears stream down my cheek as I keep pulling to get away.

'Where am I?' I cry.

A few moments pass in silence. Again, I tug to free my arm.

'Stop wriggling!' the poltergeist snarls.

'Let me go!' I demand.

Out of the darkness, a pale face appears. White, bloodshot eyes stare back at me. A gasp escapes my lips. I step back, pulling at my arm and then a scream tears through me. Squeezing my eyes shut, I mumble to myself, 'This isn't real, this is just a nightmare, and when I open my eyes I will be in my bedroom.'

When I open my eyes, the pale face is still staring at me. My body trembles as my stomach churns and my head becomes light.

'Accept you are coming with me and be quiet,' the poltergeist says, disappearing back into the dark.

Further into the darkness, we stop, and a headstone appears, my name upon it.

'No, no, that's not me. Now let me go!' I beg.

Turning my head, there is a glimmer of light in the distance. I claw at the icy hand holding me, twisting and tugging, but the grip is too tight. A laugh fills the air, drowning out the whispers.

'You will never escape,' the poltergeist declares.

I keep tugging, but the grip tightens, and I wince from the pain. Clasping the icy hand, I pull it towards me and bite as hard as I can. The poltergeist screams, and my hand is free. Spinning around, I dash towards the light.

'Horrible child. When I catch you, you'll be sorry!' the poltergeist yells.

I focus on the light in the distance and try to gain speed. Footsteps are behind me, getting louder. I quicken my pace, but it seems pointless as the poltergeist gains on me.

'Get back here!' he bellows.

As the hand tries to grab my arm, I focus on the light, keeping my arms and hands close to my body.

The poltergeist screams at me, 'Get back here! We are not done!'

The light is in reach. I'm almost there when the poltergeist grabs my arms, pulling me backwards. I want to go home, so I pull the icy hand towards me. Clamping my mouth around it, I bite as hard as I can.

'Arrrgh!' the poltergeist screams, releasing my hand once more.

I fall backwards through the light, and a whisper comes close to my ear. 'The poltergeist's name is Henry.'

The poltergeist appears from the dark, his eyes wide and teeth bared.

'Get back here, you ungrateful child!' he rages. He is almost at the entrance when it closes.

'This isn't over, Ann. I can assure you of that,' Henry hisses.

My rapid breaths continue as I stare at the spot where the portal was. As my breathing slows, I realise I'm in the living room and the telly is on. I call out.

'Hello?' Mum says as she enters the room.

She rushes towards me, pulling me into an embrace. Relief washes through me as I breathe in her perfume.

'What's wrong?' she whispers.

'I think I had a nightmare. What's a poltergeist?' I cry as the tears stream down my face.

She pulls me in for a tighter hug. 'Strange question, but okay. A poltergeist is something that creates lots of noise and causes trouble. Does that answer your question?'

'I think so,' I sniffle.

'Do you want to talk about it?'

'No,' I reply, shaking my head.

'Your imagination is very active. Maybe you should go outside and play with Lou instead of watching TV,' she insists.

Cracking half a smile, I nod in agreement. When I'm alone again, I retrieve the picture from under my T-shirt. Holding it by its frame, I observe it's a black-and-white photograph of a woman. She is wearing a light dress, and her head tilts to one side with a slight smile. Her hair is dark and sits at her shoulders. Placing the photo under a cushion, I head for the garden. When I get to the steps, I freeze.

I'd better show them the picture.

Turning around, I run back inside, retrieving the photograph. Darting into the kitchen, I show Mum and Uncle Art.

'Where did you get this?' Mum asks.

'Ann went into the attic earlier. Is that where you got it?' my uncle interjects.

I nod in agreement, taking a step back and lowering my head.

He focuses on the picture. 'If you found it in the attic, it could have belonged to a servant. Pictures could be expensive back then, so they would have had to save up for something like this. Since you found it, you can take it home if you want.'

I lift my head, beaming. 'Thank you.'

Chapter 8

The ghost tears each room apart to find anything relating to his past. However, every room is void of any such information. Sitting in Art's armchair, he drums his fingers on the arm as he stares at the fireplace, clenching his jaw as his eyes tighten. He grabs a book from the side table and hurls it across the room, letting out a groan. Storming out of the house, the ghost heads into the street. At the end of the street, cars fly past on the main road.

Opposite is a hospital, but the name isn't visible. To the right, on the same side as the hospital, is a church. He stares at it for a while, when the name 'St James' Church' pops into his head. He glances back up the row of houses, shaking his head.

'I'm not going back,' he says.

Stepping off the curb onto the main road, a smile creeps across his face, but within seconds, he disappears. Moments later, he reappears at the end of the street. He clutches his chest as he takes a step back from the curb. His eyes widening, he stares at the main road. Shaking his head, the ghost slides one foot out and touches the curb. Taking a deep breath, he brings his other foot to the edge and tries again. When he steps off the pavement, he disappears. After a moment, he is back on the pavement. His eyes bulge as his breathing increases in speed.

'No, no, no. Why can't I leave the street? I want to wander around the church!' he screams. He kicks the wall at the end of the street and growls. 'If you can hear me, tell me why I can't leave. Did I do something wrong?'

Trudging back to the house, the ghost stares at the ground. A spot of rain hits it, and he closes his eyes. A crackle of thunder and a flash of lightning dart through him. When he looks up the rain lashes down.

'Hit a ghost while he's down, why don't you? I get the message!'

***

In the living room, he snatches a tea towel from the armchair and rubs his head to dry his slicked-back dark brown hair. Throwing the tea towel back on the chair, he storms over to the mirror but the only reflection in it is the furniture. Dropping his head, he glances at the carpet as he shuffles his foot.

A stench of rotting flesh fills the air, making the ghost lift his head. The poltergeist lunges forward from the mirror, causing him to stumble backwards. He grabs the ghost by the scuff of his jacket and glares at him.

'Get out of here!' Henry seethes.

'Who are you?' the ghost asks.

Henry spits in his face and pushes him away. Narrowing his bloodshot eyes, he clenches his fist, swings a punch, and bellows an eerie laugh when the ghost falls backwards.

'Know your place,' Henry rages.

Raising an eyebrow, the ghost stares at him while rubbing his forehead. 'Do you know me?'

Shaking his head, Henry grins. 'Know your place.'

The ghost steps forward, but Henry cracks his neck from side to side, his eyes bulging. Glaring at the ghost, he growls.

'I won't keep repeating myself over and over for you. Get out of my house,' he rages, before disappearing into the night.

The words "know your place" play over and over in the ghost's mind. *What does it mean? Who is this other ghost, and why is he so angry?* There were many questions and still no answers.

Chapter 9

Out of the darkness, an icy hand reaches for Art as he sleeps but he turns over and it misses grabbing him. Henry steps into the room and glares at Art. Stomping forward, he bends down next to him.

'Get up, old man. You're coming with me!' he screams in Art's ear.

Art doesn't stir. Henry explodes and pushes him off the bed. Now awake, Art places his hands on the mattress and pulls himself up. His eyes widen when he sees a man hanging above his bed.

'I told you to leave me alone!' Art shouts.

There is no response. Art jumps when something cold passes through him. His body trembles as the cabinet swings open. He turns to see bottles flying straight at him. Just in time, he ducks, and they slam against the ground. The curtains move and panic grips him. An eerie laugh fills the room.

'It's time to come with me,' Henry demands.

He grabs Art's arm and drags him across the room. Yanking his arm free of the poltergeist's grip, Art heads towards the door. A cold hand wraps around his arm once more and stops him. He struggles to get free.

'I am not going anywhere. I told you: leave me alone!' Art shouts.

'You never told me to leave you alone. Besides, I don't listen to demands, I give them,' Henry spits back.

'Show yourself!'

'I find this way more useful.'

Two hands grab Art's shirt and pull him forward. Art grabs the hands but recoils from their icy skin. Art throws a punch into the air, hoping to hit the voice. The hands let go, and Art stumbles backwards.

'How dare you. Gentlemen do not punch—'

'This is not about being a gentleman. I don't know what game you are playing but enough!'

'Game! You think this is a game? I can assure you this is no game, old man,' Henry hisses.

He grabs Art and puts a rope around his neck, pulling tight. Realising it is a noose, Art tries to pull it from his neck, but it's getting tighter. Art gasps for air as he tugs at the rope.

'Told you this was no game and you were coming with me,' Henry says.

Choking as he tries to speak, 'Who are…' Art coughs. '…you?'

'A gentleman.'

Art struggles to breathe as the noose tightens.

'Life is so easy to take. Watching as a person takes their last breath—it's fascinating. You should try it, old man.' Henry beams.

As Art grapples to loosen the noose, a grin creeps across the poltergeist's face. Henry pulls once more, and Art's eyes widen as blood vessels burst across the sclera. The grin becomes larger, and once Art is still, he removes the noose and disappears into the night.

Chapter 10

Standing by the kitchen door, I eavesdrop on a conversation between Mum and Uncle Art.

'Are you alright?' Mum asks.

'I'm fine. I had a bad nightmare—it seemed so real, and it was vivid. Things have been happening in this house lately, and I'm not sure what is going on. However, it's been quiet the last few days, so hopefully this is a good sign.'

The tone of my uncle's voice worries me. Turning around, the ghost is standing in front of me, shaking his head.

'Children should not eavesdrop on others' conversations,' he says.

I start to answer, but he disappears.

Lou darts past. 'Are you coming outside?' she asks.

'Race you to the shed?' I reply.

'Okay.'

Outside the back door, the sun shines, its rays warming my skin as I stand next to Lou. Turning our heads, we share a smile for a moment.

'Go!' we cheer.

As we come to the end of the path, a piercing scream echoes across the garden. Freezing, we stare at each other and then glance backwards. A woman is falling from the attic window and hits the ground with a thud.

I turn to Lou and say, 'That was what I saw a few months back.'

Lou's face drains of colour. Tilting my head and looking up, I see nothing in the attic window. Footsteps scurry away from me, and when I look back, Lou is running towards the courtyard.

I rush after her. 'Lou, what are you doing?' I yell.

'To see if the lady is okay,' she shouts, glancing over her shoulder.

'Lou, she'll be dead!' I scream.

'No, she won't—and she'll need help!'

Lou is seven and thinks she knows everything, but she doesn't. Being four years older means you know better.

'Get back here, Lou!' I yell, chasing after her.

She stands on tiptoe and folds her body over the railings. Her body trembles, she gets down and turns around, staring at me, pale faced.

'Ann, there's nothing there, but I saw...' she stutters.

'I saw it too,' I say.

Lou's eyes mist over and tears start to trickle down her face. 'Should we stop coming here?'

'No, Lou. I'm going to keep coming. Sticking together means nothing can happen to us. Agreed?'

'Okay, we stick together.'

We start back towards the shed to get the bogey. Lou nudges me with her elbow, and I return the gesture. Turning to face each other, we let out a giggle.

Halfway down the path, Henry's voice breaks through the warm glow of the sun.

'Who says nothing can happen?'

Ignoring the poltergeist, we carry on towards the shed.

'We will have so much fun together. Let's play.' Henry laughs.

Pulling the shed door open, the light shines through, breaking the dust particles that float in the air along with the musty smell. I grab the bogey, but it's stuck.

Lou helps by pulling on it. It's almost free when it jerks backwards, taking us with it. The door slams behind us.

'I told you we would play,' Henry tells us.

Chapter 11

My eyes dart around the shed. A sliver of light breaks through the door, but it's too dark to make out any objects. Stretching out my arms, I wave them around and hit something.

'Don't knock me,' Lou growls.

'Sorry. Can you see anything?' I ask.

'No!'

Moving forward, something brushes against my leg. Pulling away, a sharp object pierces my leg.

'Ouch!'

Placing my hand over the area, there is a wet patch, and when I take my hand away, blood trickles down my leg. Covering the wound, I try to stop the bleeding.

'Lou, I've cut myself!' I shout.

'I can't see anything,' Lou says, ignoring my pain.

Turning on the spot, I reach out and, using the sliver of light as a guide, try to open the door, but there's no handle.

'Do you know where the door is?' I ask.

'How would I know? I've never been shut inside the shed before,' Lou snaps.

Falling silent, I look around to find anything that will help, when my sister's cries break through the air. Trembling, my heart races as my chest gets tighter.

'Someone has grabbed me. Help!' Lou screeches as Henry's laugh echoes throughout the shed.

'Let her go!' I demand.

'Did you like—' Henry starts to gloat. However, Lou's cries distract him. 'Stop your wailing and be quiet!'

Lou's cries fade to an occasional sniffle.

'Did you like the show?' Henry asks.

'Let my sister go!' I scream, ignoring his question.

'You are very rude. No manners.'

'We didn't like your show, Henry. Now let us go!' I demand.

'Never!' he yells. 'How do you know my name?'

The door swings open but no one is there. Lou and I glance at the vegetable patch and then at each other. Grabbing her hand, I drag her outside, running from the shed. Heading for the house, we dart down the path as if our lives depend on it. Henry's voice trails behind us as we get closer to the house.

'Get back here at once!' Henry snarls.

Once inside, we pass the basement, and an unnerving laugh echoes with a chilling statement. 'I will have my way.'

Entering the living room, Lou's eyes dart to me. Her face is pale as sweat trickles down it and her body trembles.

'Why is the ghost so mad with us?' she asks. 'What did we do?'

'Lou, I don't think it's a ghost. I think it might be a poltergeist,' I stutter.

'A what? Why is it mad?'

'I don't know, but when Mum asks, we say nothing.'

She nods in agreement, turning her attention to the telly. A faint sound is in my ear, and soon it becomes clearer.

'The game isn't over. I promise you.'

Ignoring Henry, I nudge my sister. She glances at me and turns back to the programme. I nudge her again.

'What?' she yells at me.

'I need the bathroom.'

Upstairs, I clean my wound, and when we're done, the ghost is waiting for us. He's standing in front of us with his arms at his sides, staring. He seems different from the other ghost, as he doesn't move. I glare at him while keeping Lou close to me.

'Your games aren't funny. Leave us alone!' I yell.

We head for the stairs, and he doesn't move.

When we're halfway down, he asks, 'What games?'

I turn back and glare at him, but Lou carries on downstairs. I stay on the step and wait a moment. I tiptoe closer to the ghost.

'Shutting us in the dark is not nice!' I yell.

'That wasn't me,' he says before disappearing.

Now I'm alone on the stairs. The air grows colder and the light fades. Terror engulfs me. My eyes dart in every direction as I rub my neck. Stuck to the spot, I wait. After a moment, nothing. I let out a sigh. Turning around, I find the pale face and white eyes of the poltergeist staring at me. I open my mouth to scream but nothing escapes my lips.

'BOO!' Henry says with a wide grin.

Chapter 12

Staring out of the window, watching people carrying on without another thought, the ghost lets out a huff. He's still trying to recall more about his past, but everything is too fragmented to be clear. A piercing scream interrupts his thoughts. He rushes out of the bedroom into the hallway and catches the spirit who attacked him trying to frighten Ann.

'Leave her be!' he shouts.

The poltergeist turns and glares in his direction. Alive, he would fear for his life, but nothing can be worse than this eternal death, trapped in this house.

'YOU!' Henry snarls back.

'You heard what I said, now go,' he says, standing his ground.

The poltergeist pushes Ann to one side, making his way towards him. Ann's eyes widen, opening her mouth, she mumbles, 'There's two of them?'

Her eyes dart from one to the other. She tiptoes towards the staircase, then bolts down the stairs.

'HOW DARE YOU!' Henry spits back.

'How dare I? You need to stay away from the children.'

Henry pokes him. The fish smell from Henry's breath is overpowering, but the ghost doesn't react.

'You are in my way, Mr Harris. My interaction with the children is not your concern,' Henry shouts.

'You know me?'

A smirk creeps over the poltergeist's face before he engulfs the hallway with a howl. 'Don't recall your life? Let me enlighten you, Richard Harris,' he says sarcastically. 'You are the bottom of the class ranks. Behold the attic, your living quarters. You are a servant. So, I don't take orders from the likes of you. I give them.'

Henry struts away, but Richard moves in front of him.

'If you know my name, then what's yours?' Richard asks.

'I don't have to answer to you.'

'I asked you a simple question, or don't you recall your name either?'

He strikes Richard with the back of his hand and pokes him with his cold finger. The room turns blood red.

'I recall everything, and this is your fault,' he spits back.

Tackling Richard to the ground, he punches him a few times, spitting in his face. Richard doesn't fight back.

'You're weak, but at least you're starting to know your place.'

Henry disappears before Richard has a chance to retaliate.

Pondering the poltergeist's words and actions, he replays the encounter over in his mind. Richard touches his lip and detects blood. Wiping it away, he straightens himself up. When he puts his hand to his mouth once again, it is dry.

He spots the children out of the corner of his eye. They stare for a moment. They don't move. Richard carries on, but he knows they're still there. Fascinated, scared or a combination of both, they carry on staring. Turning to match their stare, Richard shakes his head, and they run back down the stairs.

Chapter 13

Lou and I don't say anything as we sit at the table. The rich smell of a cooked dinner passes my nose. Glancing at my plate, my eyes widen and my mouth starts to water. Staring at each other for a moment, we give a slight nod before Lou turns her attention back to her food. Shovelling it down, she almost chokes. She taps her foot against the floor while she hits her chest. I stare at her; she pauses for a moment before she carries on, and within a few minutes, she's eating chocolate cake and cream.

I stare at my plate as the steam rises from my food, but my appetite is gone. *There being two of them in the house does explain a few things, but why have they appeared?*

Out of the corner of my eye, my uncle is staring at me. 'Ann, is the food alright?' he asks.

'Yes, thank you.'

He hesitates for a moment. Dragging his chair closer, he places his hand on top of mine. 'Are you alright? You seem miles away.'

I glance at Lou, who is still eating, then turn back to my uncle. 'I'm good.'

He lifts one eyebrow, letting out a sigh. He stares at me for a moment, lets out another sigh and leaves the table.

'You can say if there's anything on your mind, Ann,' he says.

I nod back. He smiles as he turns back to the sink. Turning the tap on, he adds, 'Lou, the same goes for you.'

She gazes in my direction for a moment. As the sun bursts through the window, she squints. Turning to Uncle Art, she meets his gaze and replies, 'I know. Can I leave the table, as I've finished?'

'Go on. I'll clean up,' he says, clearing the table.

Outside, we ignore earlier events as we head down the garden path. My hand shakes as I open the shed door. Spotting the bogey, I pull it out before something happens. Lou snatches it from me, running down the pathway.

'Give it back!' I shout.

'No, it's my turn!' she shouts back.

I start to run after my sister when a noise from behind me gets my attention. I turn around, and one of the ghosts is in front of me. Staring at each other, we don't say a word.

I let a few moments pass before asking, 'You're the friendly one, aren't you?'

He disappears without answering me. I spin around, and my sister hasn't even noticed I'm not with her. I leave her with the bogey and sit on the wall next to the roses. She pulls the bogey around the grass. Tilting my head up, I see the attic window is empty and let out a sigh. Turning my head, the poltergeist, with blood trickling from his white eyes, is standing at the entrance to the courtyard. He looks at me with no emotion, but in his hand is a knife. He swings it back and forth between his fingers with a grin that sends a chill through me.

I run to Lou, yank her hand from the bogey and pull her towards the roses, keeping a tight grip, but the poltergeist has gone. A tug on my arm diverts my attention. Lou has got free. Her eyes are narrow and her arms are folded.

'Why did you take me away from the bogey?' she demands, tapping her foot.

'A poltergeist!' I reply.

'You said about a poltergeist earlier. Don't you mean a ghost?'

'A poltergeist is worse than a ghost, Lou. I saw a poltergeist. He was by the gate.'

'Yeah, yeah.'

'I did see the poltergeist,' I snap.

'Well I didn't see anything. Can I go back and play now—*please, Mum*?'

'Very funny,' I grumble.

When we get near the bogey, it is pushing itself in all directions. We stop and stare.

'Huh, Ann…' Lou whispers.

'Yes!'

'Are you seeing the same thing as me?' she asks.

'Uh huh. Now do you believe me?'

Chapter 14

Entering the graveyard, the poltergeist stands in front of a headstone as the wind howls against the darkness.

In loving memory of
Ada Roberts
Died 16th February 1912
Aged 24

Letting out a sinister laugh, he says, 'If only they knew, my dear wife. You got what you deserved. May you be condemned to an eternity of hell for your betrayal.'

He starts to walk away, but turns back to the grave and says with venom, 'At least our son grew up without you.'

Henry enters through the front door as he has many times before. Elated, he sits in Art's chair, gazing into the fire as he plans his next move against Art and the children, when he is interrupted.

'How do you know me?' Richard asks.

Turning around, he grins like a Cheshire cat. 'How long have you been there, Mr Harris?'

'Who are you, and how do we know each other?'

He ignores the question and instead helps himself to a brandy from the cabinet. 'All in good time, Mr Harris.' He downs the brandy as if it is his first in years.

Mr Harris knocks the glass from his cold hand and harshly says, 'You stated before: the attic was my home and I was a servant. So, I will ask again, how do you know me?'

The poltergeist's grin widens. 'Tut, tut.' He comes close to Richard's face and sarcastically adds, 'All in good time. I love a sporting chance.'

Clenching his fist, Richard says through gritted teeth, 'Stop with the riddles and tell me what I want to know!'

'You remembering will be more fun,' Henry snarls back before disappearing.

Richard grabs a dining chair and knocks it over. Stomping over to the armchair, he slumps into it. He buries his face in his hands.

***

Art's eyes bulge as his body trembles. He tries to speak but splutters as Henry tightens his icy fingers around his throat. A smirk creeps across Henry's face the more Art struggles. Henry tilts his head, his smile widening as he savours the moment. Art scratches at the icy fingers around his neck, burning his hands. With each attempt, the poltergeist tightens his grip.

'I like a fighter,' he says.

Henry lets go and Art slides to the floor as he gasps for air. Henry bends down beside him and says, 'I really don't like what you've done with my room.' As Art glares at him, he adds, 'I gave you a warning to leave my home, but you have ignored it.'

'This is *my* home,' Art whispers.

Henry grips Art, dragging him to the window and pushing his body halfway through. Art's head tilts backwards and the garden comes into focus. Rain lashes at his face as he tries to scramble back inside, but Henry continues to hold him there. Art closes his eyes and, when he opens them, he's back inside and Henry is gone.

Chapter 15

It's been a few months since my sister and I saw Uncle Art. He's been unwell and needed time to recover.

As we turn into the street, the sun disappears behind a cloud and the sky is darker. Lou and I rush down the street and spits of rain land on my head. By the time the house comes into view, the rain is lashing down. Once at the door, Lou and I are soaking through. The warmth of the fire greets us as we hobble into the living room. Uncle Art hands us each a towel so we can dry off.

'Lil, did you bring a change of clothes?' he asks.

'I did for the girls because I thought they'd be going in the garden,' Mum replies.

Wrapped in our towels, Lou and I continue to shiver.

My uncle bends down. 'Would you prefer to change in here?' he asks us.

We both nod in agreement, smiling.

He turns to Mum and says, 'I'll be making hot drinks. Come to the kitchen when you're done.'

Mum towel dries Lou's hair and, after a few minutes, hands her fresh clothes. When Mum dries my hair, my head shakes all over the place. Once she finishes, my eyes see spots, so I sit still until it stops.

After we change, we run to the kitchen. On the table are two mugs of hot chocolate.

'I know I don't have much here, so when I was at the shops, I got this for you,' Uncle Art says. 'Just as well, because of the weather.'

Wrapping my hands around the mug, steam escapes as I take quick sips until it's empty. Lou and I run back to the living room and turn on the telly as we can't go outside. Sitting in silence, we are both engrossed in the programme. A scratching from above gets my attention. My eyes widen as I turn to Lou, who is oblivious. I turn back to the telly.

A click comes from behind me. I glance over my shoulder—the cabinet door shuts by itself. A glass floats upwards and tilts as if someone is having a drink. I nudge Lou.

'Not again,' she squeaks as she fidgets, rubbing her hands together.

I grab her hands so she stops, and I say, 'We'll be okay.'

The room becomes dark and cold air surrounds us, filled by a putrid smell of rotting flesh. A sharp point digs into my right side and, as I glance down, a silver blade glistens. The white eyes appear out of the darkness.

'Head to the attic and I won't use the knife,' Henry demands, pushing it harder against my side. The stench from his breath makes me sick.

Trembling, I nod. I get to the stairs, and Lou comes up beside me.

'You're not going alone,' she states.

Considering her age, sometimes she surprises me. I try to argue, but she insists on coming too. Facing the attic stairs, I close my eyes. My body trembles as I put one foot in front of the other. As I slide my hand up the banister my palm becomes clammy. I tiptoe upwards. My mind is racing as I get closer to the top. Turning the corner, the door creaks open, but there is no chair; the room is empty. I sigh with relief and smile at Lou.

Turning back to the stairs, the poltergeist with white eyes is there. Blood pours from his eyes and mouth. A tug comes from behind. Lou is trembling as she tries to hide.

'You have something that belongs to me, and I want it back,' Henry snarls as the veins in his neck pulsate.

Chapter 16

Pushing Lou inside the attic room, I close the door. Henry glides through with ease. Grabbing my arm, he tears me away from my sister. He picks her up by her jumper and carries her back to the door. Opening it, he drops her down and slams it shut.

The door handle shakes as Lou cries, trying to re-enter the room. Henry glares at me with a grin and paces towards me. I step away but he is upon me in seconds.

'Where is it?' he hisses.

'Where's what?' I cry.

His brows narrow as he tries to assess my response. His eyes burn into mine, his face right next to my face.

'I know you have it. Now give it back,' he spits. Every tooth in his mouth is stained. Some blood from his mouth splatters onto my face. I wipe it away.

'What do you think I have?' I whisper.

'You have my ring, and I want it back.'

I cross my arms, glaring at the poltergeist, and I shout, 'I don't have any ring of yours.' I raise my shaking hand and place it in front of his eyes. 'See? This is the only ring I have,' I say, showing him the small rose-shaped ring on my left hand.

He is silent for a moment, then jabs me with his finger. 'Don't lie to me. You have until the next time you visit to return the ring.'

I stare at him, tears streaming down my face as my lips tremble. I open my mouth to speak, but my words are broken by a stutter.

The poltergeist darts forward. 'Now, don't forget to have the ring when you return,' he says before he disappears.

The door swings open and my uncle rushes towards me, scooping me up in his arms. I cry into his chest.

A few moments pass and then he asks, 'What happened?'

'You have ghosts,' I cry.

Chapter 17

In the living room, my uncle listens to me explain what happened in the attic. As he paces the floor, his eyes ready to pop, Uncle Art rolls up his sleeves. Making his way to the door, he storms up the stairs. I attempt to follow, but Mum grips my arm. I tug my arm loose and dart to the bottom of the stairs. As I tiptoe up the stairs, I eavesdrop.

'What do you want with the children?' my uncle bellows.

'I want nothing from the children,' a voice answers.

'My niece was pale when I found her in the attic. She was very shaken. What did you do and who are you?'

Creeping up a few steps, I'm almost able to see who my uncle is talking to when a cough comes from behind me. I jump and glance over my shoulder. Mum is glaring at me. Her arms are folded as her foot taps the floor.

'Leave your uncle alone. I think he's just venting out loud.'

I walk back down a few steps. 'He's talking to a ghost!'

Shaking her head, she says, 'I know you say you saw a ghost, but it's your imagination playing tricks on you. This is an old house and many people have lived here, but there are no ghosts. I think your uncle is just humouring you, Ann.'

Stamping my feet on the stairs, I yell, 'There is a ghost in the house, and just because you can't see one doesn't mean it's not real!'

Mum's eyes bulge from their sockets, and as her brows narrow, I continue up the stairs before I'm dragged backwards.

'Ann, get back here right now!' she demands, but I ignore her.

When I reach the top of the stairs, the voices are coming from my uncle's room.

'You're telling me there are two of you in this house?' my uncle asks.

'It appears so, but it's only in the last few months I have become aware of him. I have no memory, but he seems to know me.'

Through the crack in the inner door, I spot the ghost standing by the window. Uncle Art is in front of him.

'Did you mess up my wife's room?'

'I did return everything to its rightful place. I want answers,' Richard says. Pausing for a moment, he adds, 'The other ghost says I was a servant.'

'If that is right then you would've had a room in the attic?'

'If what he says is to be believed, then yes.'

'My niece found a picture of a woman in the attic.'

The ghost's eyes widen. 'Where is it?'

'Ann took it home, but that was months ago. She may not even have it anymore. Also, the ghost claims Ann has a ring. Do you know anything about the ring he wants?'

Richard ignores the question. 'Get her to bring back the picture; it may provoke a memory for me,' he demands, rubbing the back of his neck.

Letting out a sigh, my uncle replies, 'I will try, but I can't guarantee she'll remember.'

He starts to walk away, but the ghost gets in front of him. 'Please, it could be vital.'

'All I can do is try,' Uncle Art answers.

When he approaches the doorway, I dart towards the stairs, and Henry whispers in my ear.

'Remember the ring, or else.'

My body trembles as I dart down the stairs. I am almost at the bottom when I hear footsteps behind me. Once I'm off the steps, I turn to see my uncle. He raises his eyebrows at me.

'I needed the toilet,' I smile.

'Without your sister? That is a miracle.'

I grin without saying a word and watch as he passes me in the hallway.

Glancing back at me, he says, 'Can you bring back the picture you found in the attic?'

I want to ask why, but instead I nod as Uncle Art walks away.

Chapter 18

It's blustery, with trees rustling against the darkness. Richard observes the poltergeist walk through the main door. He waits a few minutes then follows him. The poltergeist strides down the street, whistling to himself. Richard, horrified, quickens his pace in order to catch up. The poltergeist turns the corner and strolls down the road. Richard attempts to follow but vanishes. When he reappears, he is back at the end of the street. In the distance, he glares at the poltergeist continuing his journey.

Richard clenches his fist and cries out. 'Why can't I leave this street? Why am I a condemned man?' He grabs his head with both hands.

Letting out a sigh, he walks back to the house. Entering the kitchen, he sees Art has left papers all over the table. Richard starts to sort through the papers and comes across some old newspapers. He picks up the *Western Mail* dated Saturday 27 October 1906 and flicks through the pages. A headline grabs his attention:

New Theatre Cardiff
Mr Beerbohm Tree's Company
Date of Opening: 10th December.

***

Richard had just walked out of the newly opened theatre. Saving money had enabled him to attend— luxuries such as these are expensive but worth it.

There is a chill in the air, so he retrieves his gloves from his coat pocket, and as he puts them on, a young girl catches his eye. Although he cannot remember what she looks like, he recalls tipping his hat to acknowledge her.

He crosses the road to speak with her.

'Evening, miss.'

'Evening. Did you enjoy the play?' she asks.

'I did. I recommend the play, if you have not already seen it.'

The girl's face becomes a little clearer. Her eyes glisten in the evening light. She is about to respond, but there is an interruption.

'Young man, leave my daughter be,' says the girl's mother, folding her arms as she squints in his direction. 'She is engaged to be married, so leave.'

'Should it not be your daughter's choice to ask me to leave?' he says, maintaining eye contact.

'Insolent boy, do you not have manners? Now leave.' She swings her bag at him, catching the back of his head.

He touches the spot and narrows his eyes in disgust, but he turns to the girl with a smile.

'Hopefully, we will meet again,' he tells her.

***

Now, a smile creeps over Richard's face. If only he could have had a clear vision of what the girl looked like, but at least he knew he'd had a crush before his death.

Chapter 19

The red velvet curtains are drawn to shut out the miserable day. The stormy winds howl through the trees and the rain lashes against the window, making it seem more like winter. The only light illuminating the room comes from the glow of the electric fire and the telly.

Art is watching the news when the phone starts to ring. He can feel the cold as he enters the kitchen. Switching the light on, he picks up the receiver.

'Lil, is she alright?' he asks, his voice deepening.

Henry tries to eavesdrop, hiding in the shadows so Art doesn't notice him. He can only make out one side of the conversation and it infuriates him.

'Send her my love, and hopefully I'll see you all soon,' Art says.

After putting the phone down, Art's demeanour changes as he lets out a sigh. He was looking forward to seeing the girls. He makes a drink and, as he turns to walk out of the kitchen, a woman's body is lying on the floor. Art drops the cup, steps backwards and covers his mouth.

'I see you like my handiwork!' Henry says.

Art turns around to see white eyes staring at him. Panic grips him as he steps away, but the poltergeist keeps pace with him.

'Don't you like what you see?' A grin creeps across Henry's face.

Stuttering the words, Art answers, 'You did this?'

Henry's smile widens as he nods. 'She had to go!'

Art steps back and knocks the chair behind him, making him jump.

'I enjoy my work.' Keeping eye contact with Art, Henry adds, 'Choking you was fun, but I want to know about the phone call.'

'Why?'

Henry darts towards Art, stopping within inches of his face. 'I ask a question and you answer. So, what was the call about?'

Art gulps but keeps eye contact with Henry. 'I was expecting visitors tomorrow but they have cancelled,' he stutters.

Henry narrows his eyes, not once flinching. 'Visitors... what visitors? I've being watching you for years and the only visitors you have are the girls. You treat them as if they were your granddaughters. So, what you mean is the girls are not coming?'

He can tell by Art's reaction that he's right. Art tries to get away but the poltergeist keeps up with him. Henry grabs him by the throat, bringing him closer so they are only inches apart.

'When are the girls coming?' he snarls.

'I... I don't know.'

'Wrong answer!' Henry yells. He lets go and asks, 'When will they be coming here again?'

Rubbing his neck, Art replies, 'Maybe in a few weeks, but why are you so interested in the girls?'

'None of your concern, but I'm not interested in the girls. I'm interested in Ann.'

Art's eyes widen as his mouth opens. Taking a step back, he stares at Henry. After a few moments, he asks, 'What is your name, and what has Ann done to you? You were born before her and me.'

A smile creeps across Henry's face. 'My name isn't for you to know, but Ann has something which belongs to me, and I want it returned.'

Art backs away, but has nowhere else to go as he hits the wall behind him. 'What can Ann possibly have that you want? She's just a child!'

The poltergeist becomes erratic. 'Enough! Now answer my question.'

The kitchen plunges into darkness, with only the gloomy weather as light.

A woman walks into the kitchen. Her dark hair is tied up and her dress is pale but elegant. The kitchen changes into a dining room. Art continues to observe, wondering if this is related to the poltergeist's behaviour. He glances up and sees a chandelier above a mahogany table. He sees a sideboard with a few decanters, and he wishes he could help himself to a drink.

The lady takes a seat, then a young girl serves her dinner and a man walks in. Art doesn't see what he looks like. The woman doesn't acknowledge him as she starts eating her food. The man stops beside her and starts arguing with her. She rises from her seat and argues back, but after a few minutes, he slaps her with the back of his hand. The maid's eyes widen, her body shaking; she leaves the room, closing the door behind her. The man puts his hand around the woman's throat. Holding her down, he lifts her dress, forcing himself on her as she screams out.

Now standing back in the kitchen, it takes Art a few moments to comprehend what he has witnessed.

Chapter 20

Art is about to leave when Henry launches himself at him. Henry tries to stab him, but Art dodges the blade. Art runs out of the kitchen and heads for the back door, but it's locked. As he tries to turn the key in the lock, it becomes loose and falls to the floor.

He bends down to pick it up when the footsteps behind him get closer. Glancing over his shoulder, he sees nothing. Turning back to the key, the steps become louder.

'You can't hide from me, old man,' Henry says.

Art is shaking and his hands are clammy. He can't grip the key.

'You weren't supposed to see that,' Henry says.

Unlocking the door, Art heads out into the garden. He runs down the wooden steps. Glancing back, he sees Henry come through the door. The wind pushes against Art, and the rain distorts his view. Halfway down the garden, the footsteps stop and the howling of the wind is all Art can hear.

He turns and the poltergeist is gone. Pausing for a moment, he tries to get his breath back. He gazes at his shirt—it's wet, almost transparent from the rain. Heading back to the house, something taps his shoulder. Art stops, the blood draining from his face. He closes his eyes, hoping he is going to wake from the nightmare, but when he opens them again, the poltergeist is standing in front of him.

'You didn't think I'd disappeared, did you?'

Panic sets in. Art's heart is racing as his eyes dart back and forth, looking for an escape. He steps backwards, widening the gap between them. Turning around, he heads for the garage. Glancing over his shoulder, he sees the poltergeist is shaking his head.

'Old man, you can't outrun me.'

Running is taking its toll; Art loses his balance and falls to the ground. The soil is muddy but he is too exhausted to move. The footsteps get closer and he turns over in the mud, ready to accept his fate.

'Finally, you are ready to die,' Henry says.

Art stares at the poltergeist's empty soul. He doesn't answer him.

Henry bends down beside him. He grabs Art's face and forces him to look into his eyes once more.

'Looking into a person's eyes before I kill them is so important,' Henry grins.

Art pulls his face away from the poltergeist. 'I won't give you that pleasure,' he spits back.

A sharp pain comes from his side and travels down his body. The poltergeist yanks Art's face back. When he tries to look away, Henry yells out, 'You will look at me while I end your life!' And they lock eyes once more.

'You want to kill me, then go ahead, but I will look away.'

This time, Art closes his eyes. The pain intensifies as Henry demands Art opens them. The poltergeist lets out an exasperated sigh, his temper increasing. His eyes narrow as he looks down at Art. He thumps Art in the chest and gleams when Art jolts, but Art's eyes stay closed.

'Open your eyes so I can see the life drain away,' Henry demands.

Art ignores him. Henry punches Art in the chest. Art keeps his eyes shut. Henry throws another punch.

'Open your eyes!'

After a few minutes, an eerie silence descends. Art lies there, waiting for the outbreak of abuse to start again, but it never comes. He opens his eyes as the rain lashes down. Moving his head to look around, all that comes into view is the vegetables and his late wife's roses.

Chapter 21

Letting the steam of the bath relax him, Art closes his eyes, sinking deeper into the water to try and forget what happened earlier.

'You were almost killed out there,' Richard says.

Art flinches as he bolts upright and opens his eyes. The ghost is sat on the toilet, and Art covers himself with his hands.

'Can't a man have a bath in peace?' Art yells.

'I save your life and you lie there and yell at me.'

Art leans forward and lets out a sigh. 'Thank you. Now leave me alone.'

'We need to talk!'

'We can talk after I've had my bath in peace.'

Richard nods before disappearing. He heads downstairs and waits in the living room. He paces the room, placing his hands in the small of his back, when the poltergeist appears in the doorway.

'How dare you interfere!' Henry seethes.

Richard's eyes narrow as he grinds his teeth. 'Go back to hell and leave Art alone.'

Henry lets out a chuckle. He jabs Richard with his finger, his eyes growing colder as he lowers his tone. 'Stay out of my way, Mr Harris.'

'Is that statement supposed to scare me?' Richard retorts.

Henry reaches inside Richard's chest with his cold hand and squeezes his heart. Richard falls to his knees, letting out a whimper as his eyes close. Giving one last tug, Henry lets go. Richard leans forward, putting one hand on his chest while supporting his body with the other.

Hovering over Richard, Henry smirks. 'Your loyalty to the old man is touching but misplaced. Your loyalty should be with your master. Me.'

Richard tilts his head towards the poltergeist and glares at him. 'Loyalty ended when we died,' he says as he gasps for breath.

Henry grabs Richard's hair and yanks his head back. 'You never had loyalty to me! You abused it. You are a traitor!'

'How am I a traitor?' Richard spits back.

'You crossed the line. This is all I will tell you. When you remember, then we will talk,' Henry mocks before he vanishes.

Richard pulls himself up and stumbles onto the sofa. Shaken, he closes his eyes for a moment. Flickers of images race through his mind. The woman from the theatre, a church tower, and then a piercing scream echoes in his head. It won't stop. The memory is so powerful that Richard screams out in pain. It's as if his heart is being pulled from his chest. He rocks back and forth, repeating the words, '*Stop! Make it stop,*' as Art walks in the room.

'Are you alright?' Art asks.

Richard looks up. 'I'm fine. Can we talk now?' he begs.

'You saved me, so it's the least I can do. After this, I want you to leave me.'

'You need to be aware: regardless of if we never talk again, I am bound to this house. I will be here long after you have passed. Do you understand?'

Art nods, and Richard speaks. 'My name is Richard Harris, and I need your help.'

'Why do you need my help? Surely there is someone on your side that can help you?'

'I wish there was someone who could help, but as I said, I'm bound to this house, and I've never seen another ghost until now. But I won't be asking him, as this other ghost is terrifying.'

Art lights the fire and sits on his chair. Staring at the fire, he says, 'I think he's a poltergeist and not a ghost. Do you know him?'

'He says he was my master, but I don't remember. I have memories but they are all over the place.'

Art sighs. 'What do you mean by master?'

'He says he was my master and that I was a servant, but I have no memory. So I don't know if he is telling the truth.'

Art lifts his head up and stares at Richard. 'What is it you want from me?'

'Help me piece together my life.' Sitting opposite Art, Richard adds, 'If I do know him. Then, with your help, he can disappear for good.'

Chapter 22

I dump my bag down on the chair and a cough comes from behind me. I spin around and my uncle is frowning at me.

'Remove your bag from the chair please. Chairs are for sitting on and not for bags.'

I remove the bag and place it by the kitchen window. For a brief moment, the heat from the sun warms my arm. 'Sorry. How've you been?'

'Busy with the garden. Would you like to help me later?'

I run back to his side. 'Yes, I'll help you. I also have the picture you asked me to bring. The one from the attic.'

He looks at me. 'When you were here last time, the ghost mentioned something about a ring. Do you know what he was talking about?'

'I don't know anything about a ring and I haven't got any ring,' I tell him.

'Ann, it's okay. I know you don't have it, but I had to ask because I have no idea what the poltergeist is talking about.'

I run towards the back door, but as I get there, something grabs my arm, dragging me to the basement. I try and scream but no sound escapes my lips. It's dark and I don't recognise anything.

Something brushes against my arm and I back away. My heart is beating fast. Trickles of sweat run down my face. My eyes dart left to right, trying to work out where I am and if anyone is with me. A glimpse of light appears in the distance, but instinct tells me to stay where I am.

In the light, a woman appears. She stumbles to a bench and cries. A man grabs her arm, pulling her to her feet. The woman tries to yank her arm free, but he pulls her in the opposite direction.

The scene changes, and the woman is at her dressing table. Her dark hair is draped over her shoulders. She gathers her hair to put it up, but her hands are shaking. Her eyes are watery and her cheeks are red. Pulling back her collar, the woman touches her bruises. She rests her head on the table and whimpers. The door swings open and a man storms in. Using the back of his hand, he knocks her off the stool. She doesn't move. He grabs her throat, pulling her to her feet. Gasping for air, the woman tries to pull his hand from her neck. Wiping the tears away, he kisses her. He grips her waist, pulling her closer, intensifying the kiss, and then leaves the room. The woman steps back, holding on to the dressing table for support.

The scene changes again. I'm at the top of the attic stairs. The man is in front of me, tapping his foot with his arms folded. The woman comes around the corner. She catches sight of the man and tries to run back down the stairs, but he grabs her arm. Shaking her, he raises his hand and strikes her. Part of her hair falls loose. Taking both her arms, he pushes her down the stairs. A smile creeps across his face as, peering over the banister, he sees a young girl helping the lady up. Once they are gone, he strolls downstairs as if nothing happened.

This time, I'm in the bedroom; the woman is being held against the wall. The man's fist is clenched.

'Are you telling me the truth?' he snarls at her.

'I swear on my life that I'm telling the truth,' she cries.

He unclenches his fist and holds her face still. He kisses her for a moment. 'If I find out you are lying to me, I will end your life.'

After he leaves, the woman sits on the bed and breaks down. The door opens and she glances up to the man.

'We are having guests later, and I expect you to behave accordingly,' he demands.

She wipes the tears away and softly says, 'I will, darling.'

Now, I'm standing at the back door. I look around, expecting to see the woman, but I'm on my own.

Chapter 23

Turning around, I run for the kitchen but no one is there. Falling into a dining chair, I place my hands on the table and bury my head. *So many questions about what I have witnessed.* Footsteps come closer to me. I glance up and the kitchen changes into a dining room. I squeeze my eyes shut and open them again, but I'm in a dining room, still. The woman from the other visions appears, but this time, she walks into the room with a smile. A man is in front of her, and from behind her back, she pulls a present. I try to get a view of the man's face, but he moves.

'Happy birthday. I'm sorry it's not much,' the woman says.

I don't hear the response, but she wraps her arms around him and whispers in his ear.

The door opens and a maid walks in. 'Sorry, miss, but your husband is walking up tha street.'

The woman's eyes turn dull as the man leaves. She grabs his hand. He stops but doesn't turn around.

'Be careful,' she says to him.

They stay still for a moment, and I don't know if he is talking to her. Once she lets go, he leaves the room. She looks in my direction and smiles. The kitchen returns, and I'm sitting on my chair.

Did she see me or was she looking out the window?

My uncle walks into the kitchen.

'Are you coming outside to help in the garden?' he asks me.

I jump up out of the chair and run past him.

'I'll take that as a yes,' he says.

Over the next few hours, I gather various vegetables from the garden using carrier bags and dishes. After all the vegetables have been collected, I stay outside while Uncle Art plants seeds.

My sister comes running down the path, almost knocking me over. 'Look what I got from the shop,' Lou says as she points to her new shoes.

'Nice shoes,' I reply.

As Mum and Uncle Art talk, my sister gets distracted and wanders into the vegetable patch, weaving between the cabbages. When she comes out the other side, back onto the path, Mum shouts, 'Lou! Those are new shoes, and now they're covered in mud!'

Lou puts her hands behind her back, swinging slightly left to right with a pout. 'I'm sorry,' she replies in a low tone.

My mum frowns at her, shaking her head as she walks away. A grin appears across my sister's face.

'Girls, take the vegetables into the house, please, before the rain starts,' Uncle Art tells us.

We grab a bowl each and make our way back to the house. I get to the balcony, and Henry says, 'I want my ring.'

I run, dropping the bowl, but my sister catches it. My body is shaking, so Lou takes the bowl into the kitchen.

'Where is the ring?!' the poltergeist yells.

I dart for the living room, but a cold hand grabs me and drags me up the stairs. Lou tries to pull me down, but she isn't strong enough and falls backwards.

Chapter 24

Lying on the floor of a small room, my head hurts. I lift it to scan the room and realise I'm in the attic. Getting to my feet, I wander towards the door. My breathing becomes shallow as I become more aware of my surroundings. I reach out for the handle and go flying backwards, hitting the wall and sliding to the floor. A throbbing pain starts as I touch the back of my head. However, no one is in the room. It is eerily quiet.

My body aches as I force myself up. I watch as a piece of chalk starts to draw. As the drawing takes shape, my heart beats faster. I run for the door, but a force knocks me to the floor again. I recognise the symbol; it's a pentagram. The room becomes darker. I glance up and the ceiling is black. Candles appear. My stomach knots as nausea takes over. Teenagers are at each point of the pentagram. They begin to chant when a girl breaks from her position to have a drink. The others yell at her. She bends down and picks up something off the floor. A smile creeps across her face.

'Maybe this will help when we chant,' she says.

'What is it?' her friend asks.

'A battered ring.'

The ring is eighteen-carat gold. In its rectangle setting, there are a few tiny diamonds and a large sapphire, but there are two empty slots and their stones are missing.

'Cool. I wonder what it can do.' another friend says.

They start chanting, and the girl holds up the ring. The window smashes. Glass is everywhere. They keep going as the wind howls through the room. Suddenly, the candles blow out and they all start to scream. The candles reignite and the screaming stops. They are all nervous and on edge but relieved. A boy lets out a laugh.

'Told you nothing would happen,' he says confidently.

'The window wasn't supposed to smash,' the girl insists.

'The owner probably hasn't updated the window. It's just the weather.'

The boy is still talking but the others have stepped back. They've gone pale and are shaking. A ghost comes through the wall behind the boy. It's Henry. He whispers something to the boy, who spins around.

'BOO!' the poltergeist taunts.

The boy tries to step away from him.

'Where is my ring?' Henry bellows.

They all look at each other, but no one says a word. The poltergeist gives them a warning. I notice the girl drop the ring and kick it backwards. One of them heads for the door, but Henry gets there first.

'No one is leaving. Now where is the ring?' he yells.

They all glance at each other and back to the poltergeist. It isn't long before they give up their friend. Henry comes really close to her and holds out his hand.

'I... I... threw it away,' she stutters.

He lashes out, starting with the boy. Invading the boy's space, he says, 'Just so you know, something is going to happen tonight.'

He grabs him by the throat and squeezes. The boy kicks his legs in the air as he tries to free himself. He wheezes as the grip becomes tighter and the poltergeist's laugh echoes around the room. After a few minutes, the boy no longer struggles. The ghost lets go, and the boy's lifeless body hits the floor. The screams fill the attic as he approaches each teen in turn.

He puts his hand into a girl's chest and squeezes so hard she falls, lifeless, to the floor. Another, he throws out the broken window. Her screams fade until her body hits the ground with a thud.

Now, I cower in the corner as the room brightens up around me, the sun shining through the window. The poltergeist strolls towards me, and the room turns a blood red.

Chapter 25

Standing in front of me, Henry lets out a sigh. His icy, pale fingers wrap around my throat as he drags me to my feet. A putrid smell of death surrounds him, and as he lets me go, slime lingers on my neck. I try to rub it off.

'Why did you kill them?' I cry.

He pulls at his jacket sleeves, ignoring my question. 'Now you know what I am capable of, I would take that as a warning. Now return my ring!'

'I don't have your ring, Henry!' I cry. 'You are a cruel person, and I want to leave.'

Inches from my face, he says, 'How do you know my name?'

'I… I... don't remember,' I stutter. 'But it is your name, isn't it?'

His lips curl up into a smile as his eyes narrow. He pokes my chest with his cold finger and says, 'No matter. I just want my ring back. If you don't have it then ask your uncle, but you will return it, and as a reward, I will spare your life.'

After the poltergeist disappears, leaving me alone in the attic, I sprint down the stairs to find Uncle Art. I find him in the garden, tending to his vegetables. Running towards him, I call out.

'Uncle Art!'

Lifting his head, he raises his eyebrows in my direction, putting down the spade.

'Ann, what's wrong?' he asks.

'Henry, the poltergeist, wants his ring back and says you know about the ring,' I babble.

Uncle Art bends down, puts his hands on my shoulders and stares at me. He stays silent for a moment, and then says, 'I think you had better start from the beginning.'

We stroll down the path and sit on the slate wall which sits a few feet up from the rose bushes.

'Ann, start from the beginning.'

Taking a deep breath, I explain what happened. Listening to me, Uncle Art doesn't interrupt. When I finish, he starts to ask questions.

'So, let me get this straight. The poltergeist is named Henry, and he thinks I know about a ring?'

'Yes,' I reply.

'He showed you that he killed a group of children—is that right?'

'Yes, Uncle Art. Is it true about the children?'

He squeezes my hand. 'Yes,' he whispers. Glancing at the house, he takes a deep breath and explains. 'I lived across the road at the time and was in the middle of buying this house. The lady that lived here was away. The first I heard of a break-in was when there were police in the street. No one knew what happened to the children, and the theory was they turned on each other and one had a heart attack. Many in the street had their doubts.'

My eyes widen as I pull my head back. 'When did it happen?' I ask.

'1972 or '73. Something like that. A few months later, your aunt and I moved in. I got rid of the pentagram and turned it into a sewing room for your aunt.'

My mouth falls opens. He stares at me, waiting for a response. A few moments pass before I manage to get out, 'No!' Uncle Art raises an eyebrow, and I add, 'Did she know?'

'No. I told her the junk room was where it happened. It probably explains why she kept saying the house was haunted. I don't know what ring he is talking about, but I'll ask the other ghost.'

'Did you show him the picture yet?' I ask.

Smiling at me, he says, 'Not yet but I will. Now go inside—your mum is waiting for you.'

Chapter 26

Later that evening, Art finds Richard in the kitchen, staring out into the garden with his arms folded.

'A penny for them,' Art says.

Richard turns around and falls into the chair by the window, resting his chin in his hand. 'I still only have fragments. One was a memory of a girl outside the New Theatre and her mother hitting me with a bag.'

Art sits in a dining chair and lets out a laugh. 'Those were the days.'

Richard raises his eyebrow as Art continues, 'Ann brought the picture.' Moving some papers, he retrieves it and slides it across the table. Richard picks it up as Art adds, 'It was found in the attic.'

Richard stares at it for a few moments. He runs his hands over the picture. 'She is the one from the theatre. Her name is...' He keeps staring, deep in thought, and blurts out, 'Her name was Ada.'

'Do you remember anything else about her?'

'Nothing. It is so frustrating. Why can't I remember?' Richard slams the picture on the table.

Art leans in closer. 'It will come back to you, but at least we have a name. I can find out if Ada lived here.'

'Thank you, Arthur. I would really appreciate it.'

'Now I need your help. The poltergeist is after a ring. Do you know why?'

Richard's eyes narrow as he leans forward, matching Art. 'I don't know. Why do you ask?'

'He showed Ann some children chanting as they held a ring and then he killed them all. Ann also said his name was Henry.'

As Richard pulls himself out of the chair, the room grows cold. His nostrils flare as he shakes his fist.

'What is it, Richard?' Art asks.

Pacing the floor, Richard scratches his forehead and glances out at the garden again, putting his arms in the small of his back. 'The roses are really beautiful at this time of year...'

'Richard, what is it?' Art yells.

Richard turns to face him. 'The lady of the house was away when I heard them force the door. I tried to communicate with them so they would leave, but they didn't hear me. When they started to chant, I left the house because it didn't sound good—'

Art interrupts. 'It's been over a decade since the children died, and in one of our early conversations, you said you didn't know about Henry until recently.'

'I spoke the truth. He only showed himself in the last few months.' Richard slams his fist against the counter. 'Ghosts can hide from each other. Remember, we have eternity, so we can take our time to plan.'

'Did you see the children's ghosts?' Art asks.

Richard takes a deep breath. Rubbing the back of his neck, he says, 'No, I did not. Just their bodies. The lady of the house was distraught. I can't believe you moved in here after that.' Richard sighs.

'The deaths went unexplained and I wanted a bigger place. Did you die in this house?' Art asks.

Richard turns away from him. 'Yes, I did. Well, I assume so, because I haunt the house.'

'Was it in your sleep?'

Ignoring the question, Richard says, 'I need to leave. Can I keep the picture?'

Art narrows his eyes, tilting his head. Letting a smile creep across his face, he says, 'Yes, and hopefully you will remember more about your life.'

Chapter 27

Closing the shed door, I turn around to find I'm no longer in the garden. I'm back in the house, but it's different. In front of me, glimmers of light shine through the crack in the door. Tiptoeing towards it, there is an eerie silence.

I walk through the door, into a light and airy room with a double bed and an oversized headboard. In between the windows is a small oval table, bearing a hand-cut crystal vase with an assortment of flowers in it. The dark green curtains drape down to the floor. A rectangular dressing table is in the corner with an oval handheld mirror and a brush on it.

I turn to leave, but words appear in red capital letters on the wall.

DO NOT LET HENRY WIN!

As I run to the door, it slams shut. Out of the corner of my eye, a pen is scribbling another message. I turn to read it.

DO NOT GIVE HIM THE RING.

I run through the door. Now, I'm back in the garden. I look around—no one is with me.

Heading back to the house, a familiar voice vibrates around me.

'Do you have my ring?' Henry demands.

I spin in a circle as the yellow and pink roses move out of view. Nothing is there. The lettuce and blackberry bushes blur into one as they leave my sight.

'I don't know what ring you're on about,' I cry.

'You are lying to me!' Henry yells.

Clenching my fists and stamping my feet on the floor, I yell, 'What ring are you going on about?'

A putrid smell passes my nose and my stomach churns. Moments later, Henry appears in front of me, his white eyes glaring. 'The ring has diamonds and sapphires.'

I rub my forehead as I meet his gaze. 'Um, what are sapphires?'

He rolls his eyes. 'Don't you know anything, child? Sapphires are a blue colour. Now where is the ring?'

I bite my lip as I glance around the garden. 'Um, I haven't seen the ring, and I'm too young to have expensive jewellery.'

Henry grabs my arm and comes close to my face. The stench of his breath makes me heave, but I force the bile back down to my stomach.

'How dare you cheek me!' Henry snarls. 'Have you no manners? Now, I want the ring.'

I pull my arm from his icy fingers. 'I don't have your stupid ring. You are horrible, so leave me alone!' I shout.

His eyes widen and his nostrils flare. He raises his hand, clenching his fist. A gust of wind pushes past me, knocking me to the ground. It scoops up Henry, dragging him backwards. Struggling to get free, he screams, 'Let me go!'

My eyes widen as Henry lowers his head, glaring at me. A smirk creeps across his face, which sends shivers through me.

'I'll be back for the ring, Ann,' Henry taunts, disappearing through the wall at the end of the garden.

Chapter 28

Fixating on the wall, I pull myself up from the floor, brushing the dirt from my clothes. Spots of rain start to fall, breaking my stare. I turn around to find Uncle Art staring at me, his brows drawn together.

'Ann, are you alright?' he asks.

Shaking my head, I begin to tremble. 'The poltergeist was here. He still thinks I have the ring. He said it was a diamond and sapphire ring. Uncle Art, how can I give something that I don't have?' I cry.

I walk towards him and he wraps his arm around me.

Heading back to the house, he says, 'I don't know. Now, come back inside. Dinner is ready and Lou wants to finish so she can have her dessert.'

We're strolling across the balcony towards the back door when Henry whispers in my ear. 'Get the ring.'

In the kitchen, I move my food around the plate.

Henry continues to taunt me in my ear. 'Where is my ring?'

Ignoring him, I scrape some food onto my fork and force it in my mouth.

'Don't ignore me when I am speaking to you!' Henry yells. 'I'm warning you.'

I slam my fork onto the plate and jump up, pushing the chair backwards. I sprint out of the kitchen, ignoring Mum calling after me. As I enter the hallway, it changes around me.

The woman is coming at me. She glances back, and when she faces me, her eyes widen and her lips tremble. Running up the stairs, the man grabs her arm, dragging her back down. He shakes her. He raises his hand and strikes her across the face. She stumbles back into the bannister. He drags her to her feet, and her hair falls past her shoulders. Letting out a whimper, she tries to steady herself. The man glares at her and pushes her to the ground, kicking her several times in her stomach. She tries to protect herself, but he is relentless, and after a few minutes, he stops and straightens his jacket, leaving her on the floor. The maid rushes from the basement and helps the woman up.

Henry appears in front of me. 'Do you have the ring yet?'

Panic sweeps through me as I step backward. 'No, and I did ask. Why do you think I have it?'

Henry folds his arms as he clenches his jaw. Through gritted teeth, he says, 'The ring was here in this house, and then it disappeared. On that day, you were the only visitor!' he seethes. His eyes grow cold as he steps closer and pokes my chest with his icy finger. 'The ring belongs to me, and I want it back!' he shouts.

His eyes begin to bulge as he bares his yellow teeth.

The room changes once more and Henry disappears. This time, the woman is staring at a ring when an older woman walks in the room.

'That is a beautiful ring, my dear,' the older woman says.

The young woman turns to her and sighs. 'I'm not sure, Mother.'

The mother scoffs at the statement. 'My dear child, he wants to marry you, be grateful. Men like him are hard to come by.'

'I understand, but there is something about him. I mean, he has never said he loves me.'

Her mother shakes her head. 'Why are you so fixated on love? Ada, please tell me you're not seeing that boy!'

The woman gets up and comes closer to her mother, 'He was sweet and charming…'

'Enough! You are engaged, and you will marry him. Understand?' the mother insists.

The woman lowers her head and, in a whisper, replies, 'Yes, I understand.'

The scene changes again. The mother is talking to a man.

'My daughter is doubting the marriage,' she tells him.

'Yes, I got that impression. She needs a firm hand, wouldn't you agree?' he says.

'Precisely. I believe the wedding should be moved up as quickly as possible.'

'Then that is settled. If you can make the arrangements, I would be most grateful.'

A smile settles on the mother's lips. The door opens, and her daughter walks in. When she glances in my direction, staring for a few moments, it becomes clear she is the woman from the photograph.

Now, I'm back in the hallway, with Mum staring at me.

Chapter 29

In the attic, Richard places the picture of Ada on the windowsill, staring at her. *How do I know you?*

However, Art's question about his death keeps repeating itself in his mind.

***

After his death, Richard found himself outside the front door of the house. Two men appeared from the house, carrying a body down the steps. The maid dabbed her eyes as they carried him towards the ambulance. An officer strolled towards her.

'Miss, can you confirm the man's name?' he asked.

When Richard tried to eavesdrop, her reply was muffled, so he didn't catch his name at the time.

The policeman rubbed the back of his neck as he tapped his foot. 'Miss, will you speak up?'

'I'm sorry, sir. I just see...' She trailed off.

'I need your statement. Now, can you tell me what you saw?' He thrust a handkerchief into her hand.

'I walk upstairs and call out for him, but no answer. I knock tha door but nothing. I enter tha room and he's swaying in tha air. Then I scream, running down tha stairs. Tha master and I comes in tha room, and he tells me to call police,' she answered.

As they lifted the body into the ambulance, the sheet came away, and Richard realised the body was his own.

***

The words '*swaying in the air*' replay in his mind. He's had many questions over the years since his death, but there is one that's niggled at him. *Why would I commit suicide?*

For the last seventy-four years, since June 1913, he has been wandering the house and its grounds, searching for answers.

He turns from the window to see Henry standing in the doorway.

'Hello, Henry,' he seethes.

'I see you know my name, Mr Harris. Do you recall anything else?' Henry asks.

Richard's eyes narrow, clenching his fist as they both circle the room. 'The lady in the picture—her name was Ada. Did she live here?'

'Would you look... at... that! Mr Richard Harris has questions,' Henry cackles.

'Stop with the games, Henry, and tell me what I want to know!' Richard yells.

Henry crosses his arms as he chuckles. 'Let the games begin.'

Richard launches himself at Henry, but he disappears and Richard skids across the floor and out of the wall, falling to the ground below. Placing his hands on the floor, he pulls himself up and brushes down his trouser leg. A sinister laugh echoes around him.

'This is too easy,' Henry taunts.

'Just say what you have to say and stop with the riddles!' Richard yells.

'It's your fault!'

Richard clenches his fist. 'What did I do?'

'Not yet—you are doing so well on your own.'

Richard growls into the air, but there is no response. Grabbing the courtyard door, he thrusts it open and slams it shut, making his way to the derelict kitchen. Leaning against the counter, he holds his head in his hands and screams, 'Henry, you will give me the answers I want to know!'

Chapter 30

Art walks into the kitchen, placing piles of papers from the library on the table. Clicking the button on the kettle, he sits down, looking over each pile. One contains information about the house while the other holds information about its previous residents. He spreads a pile out across the kitchen table and starts to scan through the papers. The kettle button pops and Art strolls over to the counter to make a cup of tea. Taking the mug back to the table, he sits back down and stares at the papers.

Shuffling through them, it becomes clear that, at the time, many women had the name Ada. Picking up a list of every Ada living in Cardiff at the turn of the century, Art disregards it. Many of them either lived in a different part of Cardiff or on another street.

When Art glances to the floor, there are streams of papers surrounding him. Letting out a sigh, he once again sorts through the papers.

In 1904, the house, 13 Cherry Avenue, had finished completion. It was placed on sale and was purchased by a man, John Roberts.

Art scans other papers, but there is no mention of this man anywhere. Scratching his forehead, Art continues his search, and as the night draws on, more papers end up on the floor. He is about to disregard another piece when an article stands out:

Woman Jumps to Her Death

In Cherry Avenue, the body of a woman was found in the courtyard this morning. The woman, who has yet to be identified, is believed to have jumped to her death. However, police are investigating the matter.

A pile of papers to his right are newspapers from the beginning of the century. He scours each one, throwing those with no relevant news to one side.

Art glances at the clock; it is one in the morning, but he has to know. Almost at the bottom of the pile, he wonders whether he will ever find out anything about the woman named Ada. With two more newspapers to go, he takes a deep breath and picks up the next paper. The headline reads:

Woman Who Jumped Is Named
The woman who tragically jumped to her death in Cherry Avenue has been named as Ada Roberts. She had recently miscarried and this is said to have led to her sudden death. Her husband is said to be distraught at her passing. She leaves behind a six-month-old boy. However, the police are treating the death as suspicious and are interrogating a possible suspect. They are appealing for anyone with information to contact them.

Art drops the paper on the table, placing his head in his hands. His mind races with questions. Wearily, he picks up the last of the newspapers and scans through it, but there is no new information about Ada's death.

Art sets it down and picks up the paper reporting her death. It is dated 18th February 1912.

Leaving the paper on the table, Art takes himself to bed.

Chapter 31

In the morning, Art walks into the kitchen and finds all the papers in neat stacks on the table. Turning towards the window, Richard shakes his head.

'Do you have any respect for your home?' he asks.

Art rolls his eyes and heads to the kettle. 'I gathered information from the local library for your benefit and was up until the early hours, so don't talk to me about how I keep my house,' Art snaps.

Richard brushes his hands through his hair and lets out a sigh. 'I'm sorry—it's just frustrating when you can't remember your life before death.'

Art makes his tea and sits in front of the large window. 'I think it's time to tell me how you died, and then I will tell you what I found.'

Taking a deep breath, Richard leans forward and says, 'All I remember is standing at the front door. The maid was crying as they brought a body from the house. The sheet blew off and I saw myself, dead! The maid said I was "swaying in the air". I took that to mean I committed suicide, but I went to church every Sunday and it's a sin. The big question is, did I commit suicide, and if so, why?'

'And you can't remember any of this?'

'Not a thing. Not even the year I died. Now, what did you find out about Ada?' Richard says, hopefully.

'I found out Ada committed suicide. They said her husband was distraught, but the police were suspicious.'

Richard raises an eyebrow, tilting his head. 'Why were the police investigating if she committed suicide?'

Art let out a sigh. 'I couldn't find any more information, other than the date of the news article, which was 18th February 1912. Does any of this ring a bell?'

Richard shakes his head, 'None of this rings a bell, Art. Are you sure there wasn't anything else?'

'Um, yes. Her name was Ada Roberts, if that helps you?'

'I wish it did, but nothing you have said has triggered a memory. Why am I here in this house? What did I do wrong?' Richard slams his fist on the table.

Art rubs his chin and says, 'I'll do a bit more research on Ada. Also, I'll see if there is anything about you. Do you have a surname?

'The poltergeist calls me Mr Harris. So, I guess you will be looking for a Richard Harris, but I have no idea if that was my real name in life. He could be lying.'

'True, but why lie about your name? What would he have to gain from that?'

Looking out the window, Richard says, 'I don't know, but I don't trust him. Did you look up the name Henry as well?'

'Do you know how many men with the name Henry there would be in Cardiff?'

'I'm sure a fair few, but at this address, Arthur, not in the city as a whole,' Richard snaps.

'Don't have a go at me!'

Ignoring Art, Richard says, 'Cardiff became a city in 1905.'

Art's eyes widen. 'Richard, what did you just say?'

Richard turns to him, narrowing his eyes, and repeats his statement. After a moment, he says, 'I remembered something.'

Chapter 32

I stroll into the living room, and on the dining table there are stacks of newspapers. I throw my bag on the sofa. My nose wrinkles as dust goes up my nostrils. I lean against the back cushion, it is hard and rough against my elbows. I rest my chin in my hands and stare out the window. A small private school is opposite. The wind whistles through the trees as children battle to get to school on time. My lips curl as I relish in the notion that Lou and I are on half term and they still have school.

Lou lies on the floor with her eyes glued to the telly. Footsteps stop behind me.

'What did I say about bags and chairs?' Uncle Art asks.

Glancing at my bag and back to Uncle Art, I lower my eyes. 'Sorry, I'll remove the bag,' I say. 'Did you show the picture to the ghost?'

'Yes, I did,' Uncle Art says. 'Her name was Ada.'

'That's an odd name.' Glancing back at the table, I ask, 'Why do you have so many newspapers?'

'I'm doing research to find out some more information about Ada.'

My eyes widen. 'Oh, did you find anything out?'

Uncle Art shakes his head. 'She died in this house—'

Lou gazes up from the telly. 'She died in this house? Then why haven't we seen her?'

'Honestly, Lou, I don't know.'

Grabbing Uncle Art's hand, I tug him towards the door. He follows me and, in the hall, asks, 'Ann, why did you pull me?'

'I didn't want Lou to freak out,' I say. 'The last time I was here, I saw writing on the wall—'

'And?' my uncle interjects.

'It said don't give him the ring and don't let him win.'

'When was this?'

My head drops as I stare at the floor. 'Just before the poltergeist turned up.'

A knock comes from the door, interrupting our conversation. Uncle Art answers the door and Mum's standing there.

'Did you get everything done?' Uncle Art asks.

'The jewellers said it wasn't ready yet, but they showed me it almost complete,' Mum replies.

'I'm surprised they could do anything with it.'

'The diamonds and sapphires are going to be stunning, and I can't wait to wear it.'

My body goes numb with the words. 'Mum,' I say. She looks at me, smiling. 'What jewellery is it?' I ask.

'Uncle Art found a bashed ring with stones missing, and I took it to be fixed.' I start to tremble, and Mum tilts her head, her mouth slightly open. 'Ann, what's wrong?'

Stumbling backwards, I bash into the wall behind me. I blurt out, 'You have the ring!'

'Yes, I know.'

Uncle Art's eyes close. He rubs his forehead. 'Lil, I know I gave you the ring, but I may need it back.'

'What? No!' Mum yells.

Uncle Art's eyes widen, popping almost out of their sockets. 'Lil, don't ever speak to me like that. Remember who you are speaking to.'

Mum's cheeks redden and she glances at the floor. 'Sorry—it's just it's really beautiful.'

As they talk, a cold hand grips me and drags me away. I scream for help but no words escape my lips as I'm hauled outside.

Chapter 33

The hand slams me against a wall. I slide down it, trying to catch my breath. The icy hand drags me up by my throat, the only thing in view is the roses. A putrid smell hits my nose as I'm in mid-air. White bulging eyes appear in front of me. Henry's back.

'Where is my ring?' he shouts.

'I don't have it,' I squeak.

He tightens his grip, baring his teeth. 'If I squeeze any tighter, you'll be dead.'

Grabbing his icy fingers, I try to prize them from my neck, but all he does is laugh at my attempts. My eyes grow heavy, starting to close. As I struggle to fight, a faint outline appears behind the poltergeist. Shutting my eyes, my body grows light as I fall through the air.

Opening my eyes, I'm in a dining room. A man has his back to me as he stares out of the window. His foot is tapping and he makes a fist. I can't see his face, so I glance out of the window. Ada is talking to a man. Her smile beams across her face as he lifts her hand and kisses it. Her eyes glisten as she lifts herself and kisses his lips. The tapping of the foot gets faster until a glass shatters over the floor. The man storms out of the kitchen, slamming the door shut.

The room changes around me and I'm in a bedroom. Ada is on the floor, curled in a ball. The man is standing over her, screaming.

'Don't deny it! I saw you, holding hands and kissing,' he says.

She keeps her face to the floor but whispers, 'I'm sorry. It won't happen again.'

'You're right, it won't. So take this as a warning.' He turns his body while kicking her in the stomach. 'Let's hope if you were expecting, you aren't now!'

She wails, tears streaming down her face, as the door slams shut. I rush over to her, but I'm dragged backwards and I'm once again in the garden.

Henry bends down next to me. 'How are you able to see my memories?' he asks. 'It doesn't matter, anyway. You'll be dead soon.'

He places his cold fingers around my throat. I clasp my hands over his fingers, but the grip is too tight. My eyes widen as my breaths become shallow. My body becomes rigid as I struggle to breathe. Henry's lips curl into a smile.

'No ring, no life,' he says.

My eyes close when suddenly the grip loosens. Voices echo in the background. I open my eyes while catching my breath. The two ghosts are fighting. Now on all fours, I cough a few times and race for the house.

Mum's eyes widen as I enter the kitchen. Darting towards me, she grabs my arms. 'You look awful,' she says, touching my forehead with back of her hand. 'Your skin is clammy—'

Brushing her hand away, I say, 'I'm not ill. The poltergeist—'

'Ann, stop this,' she snaps. 'There are no ghosts.'

'Lily, there are ghosts in this house,' Uncle Art interjects.

Mum glances at him, then at me and Lou. Uncle Art and I nod in agreement.

She tilts her head and her eyebrows draw closer together as she stares at Lou. 'Do you have something to say?'

'It can't be real,' Lou says. 'I must have had a bad dream.'

'Lou!' I shout.

A hand grabs my shoulder. I turn around and Uncle Art shakes his head at me. Ignoring his plea, I glare at Mum.

'Mum, the bad one thinks I have his ring, and he is real,' I insist. Then my eyes dart to Lou.

Mum stumbles back into the chair, looking at Uncle Art. 'The ring you gave me?'

He nods. 'Don't bring it back here. Just keep it far away from the house.'

Staring at me, Mum asks, 'Aren't you afraid, Ann?'

'I am, but I don't want to stop coming here,' I tell her.

'Lou, what about you? Mum asks.

Lou opens her mouth to answer, but we jump as the kitchen plunges into darkness. A gust of wind howls around us as Henry's voice echoes.

'This isn't over! You will give me what I want!'

Chapter 34

Mum interrogates us about the events going on in the house. As we explain, her eyes widen with horror.

'Right. I'm sorry, girls, but I think it is best we don't come to the house anymore,' she says.

'What?' I yell. 'No way—that's not fair! Why? Because of some ghosts?'

'Mum, I agree with Ann...' Lou cries.

'Enough! I have made my decision,' Mum shouts.

'Listen to your mum, girls,' Uncle Art says. Turning to Mum, he adds, 'Phone me later so we can talk, Lil.'

Touching his hand, Mum gives half a smile. 'I will, I promise.'

Lou and I drag our feet, getting our coats. Mum yells at us to hurry up and as we go to the front door, a gust of wind slams it shut. Uncle Art opens it with a smile. We try and walk through, but it happens again. The light flickers as the walls turn blood red and the putrid smell of death fills the air.

'The girls must stay here!' Henry rages.

Mum looks up towards the ceiling, her eyes darting round the narrow passage towards the front door. 'Who said that?'

'It's Henry, the poltergeist!' I shout.

Mum grabs Lou and me, stretching her arms around us. 'We are leaving!' she cries.

Pulling us closer to the door, she turns the handle and tugs, but the door doesn't move. Mum tries again, but Henry bellows in her face.

'You are not taking the girls!'

'I am taking the girls home, right now!' Mum screams.

She pulls at the door while Lou stamps her feet, tears running down her cheeks. 'You are not real! Go away.'

I try to help Mum, but something knocks me backwards. I slam into the door behind me, sliding to the floor.

When I glance up, the hall is empty, and has changed. The walls are now blue and gold, filled with an eerie silence. After a few moments, blood-curdling screams echo throughout the hall as footsteps rush down the stairs. Ada is bolting for the front door, but as she turns the corner, she falls. A man catches up to her. He has his back to me and is hunched over her. He raises his arm and strikes her; she whines in pain with each one. Once he is done, he straightens his jacket and wanders upstairs. Picking herself back up, Ada wipes her face and brushes her loose hair back. The blood trickles past her lips as she stops the bleeding with a handkerchief.

Now, I'm back in the hallway as I'm forced to my feet by Uncle Art. The door is open, and I dash outside. The door slams behind me. A chill runs through me as I get to the front gate. A cold hand grabs my arm.

Henry's chilling voice echoes in my ear. 'You are staying here until I get that ring.'

I tug my arm loose and run but his gory face appears in front of the gate. Lou is yelling for me to hurry up. She comes to the gate and he grabs her. Lou's distressing screams go through me. I bolt towards her and tug at her arm.

She is shaking her head and repeating, 'This isn't real, it's just a dream... This isn't real, it's just a dream...'

'Lou, this is real, so fight him!' I scream.

He smirks at me. 'You won't win.'

Lou's eyes narrow and she bites him. He hisses at her but she kicks him and runs down the street. Henry glares and lunges at me, but I duck and he misses. He growls at me as his glare intensifies. I run down the street to catch up with Lou. He follows us.

'Get back here! I give the orders. Do as I say!' he rages.

He keeps terrorising us as we run. Halfway down the street, his cold, icy hand grabs my leg. I turn and a smirk is across his face.

'You are coming back to the house,' he demands.

I yank my leg and trip but regain my balance. Henry still has a hold of my leg; I stop and try to free myself as he tries to drag me back towards him.

'Got you!'

I yank my leg free and dart around the corner. He tries to turn into the side street but he can't follow. I turn around to face him, and his intense gaze burns through me.

'I'll wait for you to return,' he says, as his lips curl.

Chapter 35

Henry slams the front door and storms into the living room. The smell of rotting flesh surrounds him as he taps his foot, gazing out the window. Richard stands in the doorway, ignoring the stench.

'So, there are places you can't go, Henry?'

Henry turns around; his nostrils flare as he clenches his fist. Blood trickles from his white eyes as he charges at Richard. 'I'll kill you!'

'Too late, I'm already dead,' Richards snaps back.

Henry knocks him to the floor. 'All this is your fault!'

Glaring into Henry's eyes, Richard says, 'How is all this my fault? You keep playing this stupid guessing game. So, tell me.'

Henry spits in his face. Richard pushes him off and pulls himself up. Henry grabs Richard's ankle, pulling him over and scrambling on top of him to punch him in the face. Then he lets him go. Getting to his feet, Henry brushes down his sleeves.

'Yes, there are places I can't go, but you not remembering is getting tiresome,' Henry states. 'I'll give you a hint: I knew Ada as well.'

Richard's eyes widen. 'How did you know her?'

Henry lips curl into a smile as he vanishes.

***

Richard finds Art digging in the garden, tending to his vegetable patch. There's an array of greenery sprouting up everywhere, and the fresh scent of various vegetables fills the air.

'It's for the best…' Richard says.

'Best? Lil is going to stop the girls coming here. Lou turns eight next week,' Art complains.

Richard tilts his head. 'Can't you see her?'

Art lets out a sigh. 'Yes, but…' He opens the greenhouse door. The aroma of ripened tomatoes hangs in the air as Richard follows him inside.

'But nothing; the girls will still get to see you. Besides, Henry is becoming more erratic and volatile, and keeping the girls out of the way is a good thing,' Richard reminds him. 'See Lou on her birthday and make a fuss.'

Art smiles. 'Yes, I will make a fuss. Now… how is he becoming more erratic?'

'One minute he is violent and then calm. Earlier, he launched for me and then, just as quick, calmed down. He told me he knew Ada, but the way he said it—'

'Was uncomfortable?'

'No, sinister. So, Art, be careful.'

A rattling against the glass makes Art jump. A gust of wind howls through the greenhouse, knocking a few tomato plants over. Art ambles to the glass door to shut it when his teeth start to chatter. When his lips part, his breath fogs the air, even though the sun shines through the glass.

'I think it's time we had a chat—don't you, old man?'

Art turns around to see Henry standing at the other end of the greenhouse with his hands clasped together.

Chapter 36

Art takes a step back towards the door, putting his hand behind him to grab the handle.

'I said we need to talk, so you aren't going anywhere,' Henry says as the key in the lock clicks. 'Come have a seat.' He pulls an old deck chair from the corner. His jacket appears unkempt while his face has dark circles beneath his eyes which emphasise his pale skin.

Richard stands in front of Henry, glaring at him. 'What do you want?'

The eerie silence for a moment fills the air. The stench of rotting tomatoes takes over as each plant decays. Henry's lips curl into a smile as he reaches into Richard's chest and squeezes, bringing him to his knees. Each piece of glass in the roof shatters, falling to the ground. The shards of glass surround Art, each one missing him.

Henry lets go of Richard, kicking him into a row of tomatoes. Repeating his demand to Art, he points his icy hand to the seat, urging Art to sit. Art trudges towards the chair, glancing at the row where Richard went, but it's empty.

'If you are looking for Mr Harris, he's gone,' Henry says.

'What do you want?' Art demands, stopping before getting to the chair.

Henry storms over to Art, gritting his teeth while clenching his fist. The smell of rotting flesh is overpowering, and Art covers his nose.

'Frightened, old man? You should be,' Henry spits. 'Where is the ring?'

Art steps back, but Henry keeps pace and grabs Art's shirt. 'I won't ask again.'

The stench from Henry's breath almost makes Art pass out, but he holds his breath and blurts out, 'It's not here.'

'I know that, old man. Where is it?' Henry demands, coming nose to nose with Art.

'The house is full of different items, and a few years ago I sold a few things, including a jewellery box,' Art mumbles.

Henry slaps Art across the face. As Art turns his head back to him, Henry adds, 'Let's try again, old man,' dragging him to the chair.

Art tries to get up, but he can't move. An eerie laugh comes from behind him. He turns around, and sees that Henry has a glint in his eye. A rope appears in Henry's jittering fingers. Art thrusts himself forward, but the chair topples over.

'Nice try, old man, but it's going to be a long night,' Henry says with venom.

Henry rushes forward, wrapping the rope around Art's neck. He whistles as Art chokes with each tightening of the rope.

'Remember, I can do this all night,' he says, releasing the pressure.

Art coughs as he tries to breathe and sputters out, 'Go to hell.'

'Too late, already there,' Henry gloats.

He places the rope around Art's neck once more and squeezes. 'Art, if I keep doing this, you'll be dead, so tell me what I want to know!' He releases the pressure once more so Art can speak.

Art coughs into the floor without turning his head and whispers, 'I don't have the ring, and I don't know where it is.'

'You are lying to me.'

'Why would I lie?' Art whispers.

'To protect the girls, but the only way to help them is to give me the ring.'

Art glares at Henry and spits, 'Do your worst!'

Chapter 37

Henry cracks his neck from side to side. The air grows colder as the stench turns to rotting flesh. His nostrils flare as saliva seeps from the corners of his mouth. He draws his leg back and thrusts it forward, kicking Art in the back. As his foot goes through the skin, he wiggles his shoe to cause even more terror. Art grits his teeth, closing his eyes tight as he digs his fingernails into the palms of his hands.

Planting his feet wide, Henry grabs Art's arm and squeezes. Art's eyes widen while Henry's lips curl into a grin at the excruciating pain seeping across Art's arm.

'Had enough yet, old man?' Henry beams.

Art narrows his eyes but says nothing. Henry clenches and unclenches his fist as he roars, kicking Art once more in the back. He circles Art, baring his yellow teeth.

'Answer me, old man!' he yells.

Art stares at him for a moment, then turns back to the floor, again staying silent. Henry bends down and pokes Art with his finger.

'Answer me or I will kill you!' Henry demands.

Henry grabs a plant pot from the side and throws it at Art's head, letting out a guttural roar. Art jerks and Henry's lips curl once more.

'You won't tell me about the ring? Then you need to die!' he screams in Art's ear.

Art jerks the chair across the floor, hitting a few plant pots. A crackling laugh fills the greenhouse.

'The old man is trying to get away. Not getting far, are you?' Henry snarls, kicking Art in the back of his legs. Art lets out a cough. Henry turns the chair around to face him. His eyes trickle blood as he punches Art in the chest. He grabs Art's heart and grins as Art's eyes bulge. Art gasps for air as Henry squeezes tight.

'It won't take a lot to end your life, old man. Just one more squeeze should do it,' Henry snarls.

Art shuffles his wrists back and forth in an attempt to get free. Darting his eyes around, he sees nothing that can help. All alone, he can't detect Richard anywhere in the greenhouse. The tightness in his chest makes it hard to breathe. Henry's eerie laugh echoes around them as the torment continues.

'Old man, where is the ring?' he demands.

No word escapes Art's lips. Henry's eyes widen as his fist shakes. He pounds on Art's chest several times with one hand while keeping his other hand on the heart.

'Where is that ring?'

Henry grows more erratic as the silence continues. He squeezes Art's heart more and grins as Art's eyes widen even further from the excruciating pain being thrust upon him.

Art gasps for air. He jerks the chair from side to side, but he is stuck, still.

Henry continues to squeeze his heart, and as Art's eyes start to close, Henry shouts, 'See you on the other side, old man!'

Chapter 38

Pushing the front open, I edge inside. Mum marches upstairs while Lou and I wander to the living room. She turns on the telly and I fall into the sofa. Dust particles float against the streams of light. The room is cold and uninviting without Uncle Art here.

Opposite the living room, the back door is shut and the house is eerily silent. As I glance to my left, the laundry room door creaks open. My heat races as it creaks again. I grab the sofa and grip the cushion hard, gulping as I keep staring at the door. A figure rushes by into the kitchen.

I tiptoe towards the doorway and peer into the kitchen. The tall cupboard drawer is open. Wandering into the kitchen, the nice ghost is sitting in the window, reading some newspapers.

'You don't have to creep around,' he says.

I stop and stare at him. 'What is your name?' I ask.

'Richard. How's your uncle?' he asks.

'He hasn't woken up yet. Mum says the hospital are worried.'

Richard makes eye contact with me. 'I'm sure he will pull through.'

'Did the poltergeist do this to Uncle Art?' I whisper.

Richard gives me a half smile. He places the newspaper down and takes a deep breath. 'Yes, he did, and I stopped it just in time.'

I stare at Richard as I cross my arms, then place one hand on my shoulder. 'Was he going to kill Uncle Art?' I cry.

Richard opens his mouth to respond, but Mum calls out as she wanders down the stairs. I wipe a tear away, and before he disappears, he says, 'Your uncle will be fine.'

Mum passes the kitchen and says, 'Time to go, Ann.'

I turn towards her and the poltergeist is standing next to her. He puts his finger to his lips as Mum passes him, entering the living room. As I approach the door, a smirk creeps across his face.

'I told you things would happen,' he gloats.

He grabs my arm as I step into the hallway. I glare at him. The stench of death radiates from his breath as he bares his teeth.

'Tell your uncle hello from me,' he teases.

I yank my arm free and stare at him. His grin widens.

Footsteps stop behind me, and Mum asks, 'What are you doing?'

'The poltergeist is here,' I say.

She grabs my arm, dragging me down the hall. 'There are no such things as ghosts!'

'But Mum, you saw—'

She stops and turns to me, staring into my eyes. She snaps, 'I saw nothing. I must have been tired.'

'Mum, you are deny—'

'Ann, enough!' she bellows.

Henry rolls his eyes at me as he struts towards me and Lou. 'Face it—your mum is in denial. See you soon, girls.'

As we approach the front door, it opens and Mum's hand trembles. I glance up, but she is looking straight ahead. I turn to Lou and she is shaking. Mum opens her mouth to say something but shuts it, shaking her head.

Chapter 39

A month later, I wander into the kitchen to find Uncle Art sitting on his chair by the window. The comforting aroma of a roast dinner wafts up my nose, making my stomach rumble. He starts to get out of the chair, using the cane to his left, when Mum rushes over and demands he sits back down. Uncle Art rolls his eyes, but smiles at her. Lou bounces into the kitchen, telling Mum she can't open the shed door. Uncle Art tries to get up once more but is met with daggers from Mum. I'm told to stay to keep Uncle Art company while she opens the door for Lou.

'How are you?' I ask.

'Better now that you're here,' he replies.

'Did the poltergeist really do this?' I ask.

He glances out the window as Mum turns the corner. 'Yes, he did. If it wasn't for Richard…' He trails off. 'Did Lou get her birthday present after?' he asks, changing the subject.

'I think so. Does Richard know anything more about his life?' I ask.

'I did find more information, but I haven't been through it yet.'

A knock at the door interrupts the conversation. I run out of the kitchen and open the door, but no one is there. Slamming the door shut, I make my way back to the kitchen when a thud comes from the living room. I freeze and peep through the door, seeing a book on the floor. Uncle Art is in the kitchen doorway when I wander into the living room. I pick up the book, and the cabinet door creaks open then slams shut.

'Ann, come out of there, now!' Uncle Art shouts.

I come close to the doorway but it slams shut before I can leave the living room. An unnerving laugh surrounds me as I tug on the handle but it doesn't budge. I use both hands to try and turn it, but they slide off and I fall backwards.

'Try all you like, but the door is shut,' the voice says.

I turn around and the poltergeist comes from the shadows with a grin across his face.

'I told you I'd see you soon,' Henry snarls.

Turning back to the door, I start bashing and yelling for help.

Out of the corner of my eye, Henry comes close, and when I turn my head, he says, 'Boo!'

I back away and try to keep my distance, but he keeps pace with me. I bump into something sharp. Glancing down, it is the corner of the dark brown side table. As Henry gains on me, the foul odour of rotten meat becomes strong. My stomach is churning from the stench as I go around the table. His white eyes burn into mine; he is almost on me. I hit the wall behind as he sneers at me.

'Nowhere left to go,' he says.

Grabbing my arm, he pulls me towards him. I open my mouth, but no sounds escape my lips. I try and pull away, but his cackle echoes around the room. When he pulls me right next to him, Henry disappears, screaming after me, 'Where are you going?'

I'm surrounded by gravestones. It is bleak and grey, and in the distance, a small group of people are gathered around a coffin. I come closer and hide behind a gravestone. Peeping around the corner, I see a man and woman talking, but they have their backs to me.

'I am so sorry for your loss,' she says.

He touches her hand. 'Thank you. It is a difficult time, especially with the police.'

'Do they really think it was murder?' she asks.

'They are treating her death as suspicious, and I think they suspect someone.'

A few leaves, tainted gold, orange and red, fall around me. The scent of cinnamon wafts past me as I continue to eavesdrop.

'Isn't that your servant over there?' she asks.

The man makes a fist as he storms over to other side of the graveyard.

'How dare you intrude on a man's grief!' he screams.

All the mourners stare with eyes wide at the two men. I squint at them, but they are too far away for me to identify them.

'You grieve?' the other man yells. 'More like you are happy she is dead!'

The first man launches himself at the newcomer.

Now, I'm back in the living room, face to face with Henry.

Chapter 40

Henry is only inches from my face; the stench of his breath is overwhelming, and my stomach turns as I try to stop myself from throwing up. The air is cold as the walls turn to rotting flesh around me.

'Time to come with me,' he says.

I tug to free my hand, but his grip tightens as the room grows dark. The door judders as Uncle Art tries to get inside. Henry's words fade away as I plunge into darkness. No light; only whispers and cries of suffering surround me. My body trembles, growing colder with each step. I stumble backwards, but Henry continues to drag me. I turn my head; there is nothing in the blackness. I close my eyes and open them again, but the darkness is still all around me.

As the voices become stronger, I tilt my head to the side in the hopes the sounds will fade away, but the pain and suffering still resounds through my ears. Turning my head once more, there is no escape route. Tears stream down my cheeks the further we go into the dark.

'Why?' I cry.

'I want out of this place and if I can't have the ring then someone needs to take my place,' he demands.

I try and plead with Henry. 'I don't want to be here. I'm just a kid. Isn't there another way?'

I yank at my arm, but he grips my wrist so tight I whimper in pain. I shake my head back and forth, screaming out in the hopes this will wake me up, but

I'm still here. I bend my head forward and bite his hand. He yells at me and his icy cold hand slaps my cheek. As warmth radiates through the cheek, my tears cause it to burn and swell as they slide down my face.

'Stop your snivelling,' Henry demands.

The bleak darkness is endless as Henry continues to force me through it.

'You're crazy!' I cry.

His white eyes appear from the dark. 'Is that so?' he snarls. 'I was the one wronged, and you are taking my place.'

The whispers become audible. 'Let yourself fall and we will help you.'

My eyes dart around, but they see only black. I don't know if I trust the whispers, but I'll give it a go to get away from the poltergeist. I lean backwards, allowing my legs to slide forwards, and close my eyes tight. Henry hisses at me but I ignore him.

'That's it. Try to relax,' the whisper says.

I continue to pull away from Henry, keeping my eyes shut tight, and I brush against something soft.

'What are you doing? Get up,' Henry hisses.

Ignoring his pleas, my body grows lighter and Henry's words grow distant. The softness disappears as I start falling. I open my eyes but it's still black. Henry is gone and the whispers have stopped. My stomach tenses and a shudder sweeps through my body. My heart races as I keep falling.

Am I going to die?

Chapter 41

I open my eyes to an uncomfortable darkness, but light streams through the corners of my eyes. A musty scent travels up my nose, and when I turn my head, I'm in the living room, face down on the carpet. Pulling myself up, I glance around to find I'm alone. I pat my sides to check everything is still in place. Dusting myself off, I dart for the door. I yank it open and Uncle Art is standing there.

'Are you alright? What happened?' he asks.

'He dragged me somewhere and it was dark,' I cry.

Uncle Art opens his mouth, but a knock at the door interrupts us. Hobbling, he answers it. Peeping around the corner, I see a milkman rushing down the steps. Uncle Art calls after him. I wander to the door. They are talking but the conversation is muffled. As Uncle Art turns towards the house, he shouts, 'Take care, Rich. See you in a fortnight.'

He hobbles back up the steps and closes the door behind him. I scrape my palms against my clothes, tilting my head downwards. Uncle Art stops in front of me and places his hand on my shoulder.

'Ann, I will understand if you don't want to come here again. What you have been through is horrible,' he whispers.

I raise my head, tears trickling down my cheeks. 'He's picking on you too,' I cry.

Pulling me into his chest, Uncle Art wraps his arms around me. 'We will get through this. Somehow, we need to get rid of him.'

Richard comes through the wall, and Uncle Art furrows his brow.

'I wish you wouldn't do that,' he says.

Richard rubs the back of his neck and lets out a sigh. 'Do you have any more information about my past?' he asks.

'Richard, this isn't a good time,' Uncle Art insists. 'Henry attacked Ann.'

Richard bends his head and gazes at me. He leans in, his eyebrows drawing together. 'Tell me everything, Ann,' he demands.

'I was in a dark place, and it was scary,' I say.

'Was there anything else?'

'I heard whispers and screams and… Oh, before he took me, I went somewhere else.'

Uncle Art places a hand on my shoulder. 'You didn't tell me this!' he says.

Glancing up at him, I say, 'I forgot. I was in a graveyard. There was a coffin and two men argued.'

'Did you see who they were or what they said?' Richard asks me.

Turning to face Richard, I say, 'Not all of it, but I heard one say, "You are happy she is dead." Something like that, I think. And a woman said, before the argument, that he was a servant.'

Richard opens his mouth but pauses for a moment, and Uncle Art turns to me. 'Time to go in the garden, I think,' he says.

I fold my arms and huff. 'Why do I have to go?'

Uncle Art raises his eyebrows at me, and I sigh. Turning on my heels, I mutter to myself, 'Always have to leave when things get interesting. Not fair.'

Chapter 42

Later that evening, after the girls had gone home, Richard sits next to Art in the living room as the glow of the fire lights the seating area. The rich aroma of brandy fills the air and floats up Richard's nose.

Holding the glass in his hand, Art speaks while staring into the fire. 'Help yourself; you know where it is.'

Leaning forward, clasping his hands together, Richard says, 'What is the point if you can't taste it?'

'Suit yourself. Why did you disappear earlier?' Art asks.

'Sorry about that, but with the girls here I thought it would be best to wait.'

Art turns to glare at Richard. 'Did Ann jog your memory?'

Richard pauses for a moment. 'Being at a graveyard does sound familiar, but I'm not sure. I mean, I could have attended a few funerals in my day.'

'When you get to my age, they become more frequent.'

'Did you find out more about me?' Richard begs.

Art hobbles to the cabinet and pours another brandy. Heading back to his seat, he places the glass on the side table and falls into the chair.

'I have more information but haven't been through it yet.'

Richard jumps up from the sofa with a spring in his step. 'I'll help you.'

'You are eager, aren't you?'

'Do you have any idea what it is like to not remember who you are and have snippets of memories, not knowing if they are real?'

Turning to face Richard once more, Art says, 'No, I don't. But look at me—I'm talking to a ghost and being attacked by a mad poltergeist. If anyone was to see me now, they would think I'm talking to myself or worse, gone mad.'

'I see your point. It must seem very surreal to you,' Richard says.

Art struggles to his feet and hobbles over to the doorway. He switches on the light and heads to the table. The bright light illuminates the room. He sits down and brings the pile of papers towards him.

'Are you going to help?' he asks.

Richard strolls over, takes a seat and grabs a pile.

Sifting through the paperwork, Art asks, 'What if you're not a nice person. You know, like Henry?'

Richard glances up at Art. 'Then I will know.'

'There are so many men named Richard in Cardiff,' Art says.

He looks at each paper in turn and scrolls past each name one by one with his finger, but no Richard has the surname Harris. Each turn of the papers comes with more disappointment. Then Art finds a few pages with the surname Harris.

'Too old—you'd be a baby when she died,' Art mumbles, crossing each one off in turn. 'Possible. Maybe. No, not that one.'

Richard tries to grab the paper, but Art hits his hand away.

'I think I found a few possibilities,' Art says.

'Well?' Richard demands.

Art stares at him. 'There are three possibilities. One Richard Harris had the middle name Charles, born June 1890. The other had the middle name David, born

September 1884. Finally, the last Richard Harris had no middle name, and he was born April 1888. Does any of this trigger anything for you?'

Richard scratches his head. Staring at Art, he says, 'Nothing rings a bell, but keep it to one side. Something else may connect the dots.'

Then they go back to the piles and continue the search.

Chapter 43

A gust of wind sweeps through the living room, and the papers fall on the floor. The light flickers, and the room is in darkness. A glass shatters. Art spins around, but the bleak, cold air surrounds him.

'Richard, are you still here?' he whispers.

'I'm still here.'

The door slams shut, sending quivers through Art. He rubs the back of his neck, and when he pulls himself up from the chair, a whisper comes from behind.

'Hello, old man!'

Art closes his eyes, holding his breath. His heart races, hoping this is just a dream. He takes a deep breath and opens his eyes. Out of the darkness, white eyes appear, staring at him. The hairs on the back of his neck stand up as they lock eyes. A tinge of light comes back as all three stare at one another.

'What do we have here, I wonder?' Henry sneers. 'Let me guess: Mr Harris has persuaded you to help him remember his past.'

Richard rises from the table. He snarls, 'And what does it have to do with you? After all, you know the answers and you won't tell me a thing. You attack Art and Ann, and for what? Just so you can have some fun?'

Henry swaggers over to Richard with a wide grin, crossing his arms. 'I know everything. It's a shame things ended the way they did… but it was for the best.'

Art hobbles backwards, eyes widening, as Richard clenches his fist. Richard's nostrils flare while he glares at Henry. He shoves Henry and an eerie laugh echoes around the room. Art takes more steps back, staring in horror at the two men.

The walls turn claret, darkening the room. Richard shakes as he launches himself at Henry. As Richard throws a few punches, Henry doesn't fight back. Richard lets out a growl, and Henry smirks at him. Once more, Richard raises his fist, but this time Henry grabs it, growling at Richard and forcing him off. Richard tenses his body while baring his teeth, but Henry pins him to the floor and narrows his eyes.

'Never do that again,' he snarls.

'I'll do what I like—and stay away from the girls,' Richard hisses.

Henry glares at Richard for a moment and then spits in his face. Richard knocks him off, throwing another punch. Henry grabs his cheek with his hand, glaring back at Richard. Turning his head, he lets out a roar as foam builds up in the corners of his mouth. Then he charges at Richard, throwing him against the wall.

Strolling towards Richard, a grin creeps across Henry's face. 'You will pay for that, Mr Harris.'

When he gets close, Richard smiles and disappears.

Henry turns around, brushing himself down and straightening his jacket. Staring at Art, he smirks. 'Now it's just you and me, old man.'

Chapter 44

Sitting opposite Art, Henry gestures for him to sit back down. Art keeps his eyes glued to Henry as he re-takes his seat.

'Sorry about that, Arthur. You just can't get good help these days,' Henry remarks. 'Be a good man and pass the decanter, would you?'

Art reaches behind him and fumbles around until he finds the bottle. Grabbing it, he brings it to the table without taking his eyes off Henry. Pushing it towards Henry, Art rubs his eyebrow.

'What do you want?' he asks.

Henry clasps his hands in front of his lips, tapping his fingers together. The stench of rotting flesh grows stronger, passing Art's nose. He heaves but forces the bile back down, taking a deep breath.

'What do I want?' Henry replies, pouring himself a drink. 'Good question! I want my life back, and I want the ring.'

'If you are dead, how can you have your life back? Isn't it one life and that's it?'

Henry gets up and wanders around the table, brushing it with his cold, pale hand as he sits closer to Art. Leaning forward, his bulging white eyes staring at Art, Henry taps his chin as a slight cackle escapes his blood-soaked lips.

'I was wronged in my lifetime, and now I am paying the price for something that was not my fault.'

Art backs away, his eyes widening further. His hands tremble as he folds and unfolds his arms. He bounces his right knee as the sweat trickles down his face.

'Why do you look creepy and he looks normal, if Richard is the bad guy? Surely, the beings would know who is bad and good.'

Henry snaps, 'Clearly not, or I wouldn't be here.'

'Then tell me the story, Henry,' Art insists. 'What did Richard do?'

'Tell you the story! I wish I could, old man, but it's not for me to tell.'

'Go back to hell and stay there,' Art snaps. 'I'm fed up with your bullying and stupid games.'

Henry rises from his seat, narrowing his eyes as he growls at Art. A gust of wind rushes through and knocks Art to the floor. Henry bends over and glares. Shaking his head, he kicks Art. Art lifts his head, glaring while rubbing his leg.

'Don't ever speak to me like that, ever, old man. Unfortunately, I'm not going to kill you tonight, as I have other places I need to be. However, this is not over!' Henry roars, before disappearing into the night.

Chapter 45

Art stays motionless for a moment. The room returns to normal, but the air is sombre and the silence is deafening. Pulling himself along, Art grabs the side of the dining chair and heaves himself up. Hobbling to his armchair, a musty scent hits his nose. Frozen to the spot, he hesitates for a moment, holding onto the corner of the chair for support. Turning his head, Art is alone. He falls into the chair, and a voice breaks the silence.

'What did Henry want?'

Art glances at the other armchair, where Richard appears, resting his chin in his hand.

'Thanks for helping earlier,' Art snaps.

Richard lowers his head. 'You're right—I should have stayed. I am sorry,' he whispers.

'In answer to your question, he wanted to chat.'

Leaning forward, Richard asks, 'What did he want, and are you alright?'

'He claims you are the one with a story to tell. Also, he thinks you are the bad one and he is paying the price.'

'Arthur, I'm really sorry you and the girls are suffering, but without my memories I have no idea why I'm here. If Henry is innocent then why treat you and the girls so badly?'

Now staring at Richard, Art replies, 'Honestly, I don't know. Maybe he's pissed off. I know I am!' he yells.

Richard widens his eyes. 'Arthur, I didn't know you knew such colourful words.'

'Look, Richard, I don't give a damn what you think. I just want my house back and to go back to pretending there are no ghosts,' Art insists. 'So, I will ask you once more, do you have a story to tell that will finally clear all this up?'

Leaning back in the chair, Richard rubs his chin. 'You know everything I know. The woman in the picture was named Ada. If Henry is right then I was a servant here at the house and he was my master. Do you know anything more?'

A pungent smell wafts up Art's nose. He puts his hand to his mouth to protect himself from it, closing his eyes tight. Richard's voice is still audible.

'Arthur, what is wrong?'

A cackling laugh travels around the room.

'Yes, Arthur, do tell us if you know anything,' Henry says as he steps through the wall.

Veins throb in Richard's temples; Art's hands tremble and his knee jerks. Richard rises from the armchair.

'What is it you want, Henry? For God's sake, tell us!' Richard yells.

Glaring at him, Henry's white eyes narrow and he storms closer. 'How dare you raise your voice to me—' he seethes.

'Just fill in the blanks, Henry, and go back to hell,' Art groans.

Turning to stare at Art, Henry says, 'I said it's not my story, but what I will say is that all of this is Mr Harris's fault.'

Richard steps closer, invading Henry's personal space. 'What happened here, Henry?'

'That's Mr Roberts to you,' Henry blurts out, before disappearing through the wall again.

Richard and Art stare at each other for a moment, before Art breaks the silence. He pulls himself out of the chair, hobbling to the dining table, where he starts shuffling papers on the table.

'He gave a surname, which we didn't have before,' Art says. 'Ah, here it is. A John Roberts bought the house. There is no mention of a Henry Roberts. I wonder how he is related to Ada and John?'

Richard rests his hands on the table while staring at Art. 'We need to look deeper into this,' he insists.

Chapter 46

Since Uncle Art's run-in with the poltergeist, Mum insists on having a key to the house. Lou and I run in and follow the aroma of cinnamon straight into the kitchen. The button pops as Art picks up the kettle.

'What's that smell?' I ask.

Making his tea, he smiles at us. 'A few apples fell from the tree, so I made an apple pie. Would you like some?'

We nod in agreement. I can almost taste it as I lick my lips. Lou runs and sits straight at the table in the kitchen. Tapping a fork on the table, she smiles at Uncle Art.

'I'm ready for the pie, Uncle Art!' she squeaks.

Uncle Art chuckles, but he winces as he holds his stomach. 'After dinner,' he says.

Lou storms out of the chair and across the room. Leaving, she mutters, 'Always after dinner. Not fair!'

'I heard that, Louise!' Uncle Art shouts as Lou runs out the back door. 'Go on, Ann, outside.'

I nod, and when I get to the doorway, Richard is standing there.

'Nice to see you here, Ann. Is Lou with you?' he asks.

'Yes, she is. She's run into the garden.'

'Hope you both have fun,' he replies. Turning to Uncle Art, he asks, 'What is that smell?'

Uncle Art rolls his eyes. 'Not you, too! I'm making an apple pie.'

The beaming sun hides behind some grey clouds, and the kitchen loses a bit of light. Richard relaxes and a smile spreads across his face. He bounces on his feet as he wanders to a chair. He lifts his nose, breathes deep and closes his eyes for a moment. I look at Uncle Art and back to Richard.

'It smells just like the one my mum used to make,' Richard confesses. 'She would always save me a slice after the gentry had had enough.'

I walk over to him and tap his side. He gazes at me with a smile. Bending forward, he asks, 'What is it?'

'Um, you remembered something. You remember your mum.'

Glancing at Uncle Art, his mouth widens but no words escape his lips. After a few moments, he says, 'Oh my, you are right. I do remember her. Her name was Louise…'

'Like my sister.'

'Yes, I suppose so. She was a cook for a family. I don't remember if she had a husband or if I knew my father.'

'Well, it's a good thing I cooked this apple pie, or you would still be in the dark,' Art says.

'True. However, it's all I can remember at the moment.'

'Hopefully, Richard, over time you will recall more and more,' Art reminds him.

'And I'll help you,' I interject.

'I really appreciate that, Ann. Thank you,' Richard replies.

Chapter 47

After lunch, Mum and Lou go to the shops. I sit at the table and go through the papers. The aroma of cinnamon dangles in the air as Uncle Art clears the plates.

'Find anything interesting, Ann?' he asks.

'I'm still looking. Oh, this is interesting. This picture is the same as the church down the road. The tower had scaffolding around it in 1893.'

'Interesting. Does it say anything else?'

I turn the page, but there is nothing more. Putting the picture to one side, I search through the other papers.

Letting out a sigh, I answer, 'No.'

'I remember the tower being built. I was a young boy at the time,' Richard says.

I jump in my seat and glance up from the papers. Richard smiles at me. Uncle Art sits down.

'Please tell me you have all your memory intact?' he says.

Richard lets out a sigh. 'If only that was true.'

I pick up the small pile of papers to the side. A circle around the name John Roberts grabs my interest. Lifting the page, it states he bought number 13.

That's odd, how did he know Henry?

Scanning through more papers, a gasp escapes my lips. Uncle Art and Richard stare at me.

'What have you found?' Uncle Art asks.

Glancing up from the paper, I say, 'John Roberts was Henry's dad. Here is the news article.'

Uncle Art takes the sheet from my hand and reads it.

Death of a Local Businessman

It is with sadness that a great businessman, John Roberts, dies suddenly at the age 43. John founded many charities to help the local communities. His death is being treated as suspicious and police are appealing for anyone with information to contact them. He leaves behind a son, Henry Roberts, who will continue with the business and charity work, building on his father's legacy.

Uncle Art slams the paper on the table. 'So, John bought the house and then dies suddenly and Henry gets the house. Hmm… Very suspicious.'

'You aren't suggesting what I think you're suggesting, are you?' Richard asks.

I shake my head as they continue the debate, and out of the corner of my eye, I spot the name *Ada* in one of the newspapers. In the background, Uncle Art and Richard are still in a deep discussion.

Pulling the paper closer, I read the passage. It is part of the death notices. *Ada Roberts, a beloved daughter and mother.*

Pausing for a moment, I re-read the notice. Where is the wife part?

I glance up, and I'm in a dining room. A man stands by the window with his back to me. He raises his glass.

'Well, dear wife, I'm glad you are dead,' he toasts.

I tiptoe forward and now I'm in a graveyard. The stone reads:

In loving memory of
Ada Roberts
Died 16th February 1912
Aged 24

A few people surround the coffin. They gradually disperse, leaving a man alone by the grave. An eerie smile creeps across his face. The sun disappears, leaving grey clouds above.

'Goodbye, my dear wife. If you had behaved then you wouldn't be lying in the ground,' he sneers.

Turning around, his dark hair is combed back. His cheekbones are chiselled and he is well dressed. Although his personality is dark, he struts away, widening his grin.

Now I'm back in the kitchen, staring at the notice. Uncle Art and Richard are staring at me. My eyes dart between them; Richard is the first to speak.

'Where did you go?'

I put the notice down. 'I was here, but it turned into a dining room. A man was celebrating his wife's death. Then I was in a graveyard and the man did the same thing, but this time I saw his face.'

'What did he look like?' Uncle Art asks.

'Well, he was good-looking, but he's not nice. The voice is familiar, but I can't remember from where, though.'

'Can you tell us anything more?' Richard asks. 'Did you see or hear anything?'

Leaning my head in my hand, I pause for a moment. 'The gravestone said Ada Roberts. Her death was in February 1912,' I say, picking up the notice. 'But the notice says beloved daughter and mother. Her husband was never mentioned. Did he hate her?'

Uncle Art sits next to me. 'If you saw the husband celebrating about her death then I would say he didn't love her,' he says, tapping my hand.

Chapter 48

The shadows from the trees fall over the gravestones. The stench of rotting flesh surrounds the graveyard as Henry approaches Ada's grave. He whistles along with the wind, and once at her grave, a grin creeps across his face.

'Once I have that ring back, I will be free. I should never have been sent to that place. After all, I have done nothing wrong. The house is in a terrible state. The old man has ruined it. Can you believe a kitchen now occupies the dining room? The beautiful chandelier has gone. It's disgusting that people have no appreciation for the finer things.'

Glancing to his left, Henry sighs and continues his rant. 'Look at my unkempt gravestone. I paid good money expecting my final resting place to be maintained.' He pauses for a moment. Stepping back, he stares at both gravestones. 'You are being looked after, and yet I'm being left to go unnoticed,' he spits.

Footsteps from behind cause Henry to turn around. A middle-aged man stands with flowers in his hands. A small smile lights up the man's dark brown eyes as he stares at the gravestone. Henry narrows his eyes, tilting his head. He pokes the man, but he doesn't react.

'So, you are looking after my dead wife's resting place, but you don't show me the same courtesy. Who the hell are you anyway?' he yells.

'I know we have never met, but I'm here on behalf of your son, Henry. He says to tell you he misses you every day and these flowers are for you,' the man says, laying the flowers down. 'He hopes to come and see you in the next few weeks.'

As the man leaves, Henry turns to the gravestone. His eyes widen as he clenches and unclenches his fist, his nostrils flaring.

'So, you are communicating with the living. Who is that insufferable man, and how does he know our son?' Henry demands. 'Henry better not be neglecting me after everything I did for him. The ungrateful child.'

Turning back, he notices the man get into a car and talk with a person in the passenger seat. He walks closer, but the passenger's hand covers part of their face. Henry struts over, and the passenger screams at the man who lay the flowers. The car speeds away before Henry can get there.

Chapter 49

Strolling up the stairs, Richard heads for the attic. He stares out of the window, casting his mind back to his mother and how he'd once frightened her.

The scaffolding encases the tower as the gentle breeze brushes past him while he stretches his neck. Many workmen climb up and down the ladders as the tower takes shape.

'Richard, where have you been?' a voice cries out.

He turns around and his mother is standing there, her brown hair tied in a bun and a white pin covering her long dress. Pressing her one hand to her stomach, she wipes a tear away from her eye.

'Sorry, Mother, but I was watching the tower,' Richard answers, lowering his head.

'I have to go to work, so I need you home,' she says.

Richard closes his eyes, taking a deep breath. Opening them again, he looks around and the room is empty apart from the picture of Ada sitting on the windowsill. Richard stares at the picture, willing her to come to life in the hopes she could fill in the blanks, but nothing happens. He touches his lips as a softness presses against them and a scent of rose perfume fills the air. However, as the scent fades so does any recollection. He lowers his head, resting his hands on the sill, and groans.

'What are my memories hiding from me?' he yells.

***

Art hobbles around his vegetable patch as spots of rain start to fall. A drop in temperature makes Art shudder, but he continues on regardless. Glancing up at the attic window, he notices Richard staring back. He gives half a smile, but there is no reaction. Turning back to his garden, Art shakes his head.

Putting his foot on the pitchfork, he presses down, when a blood-curdling scream cuts through the wind, making him glance up. His eyes widen in horror as a woman falls through the air, hitting the courtyard below. His mouth opens but no words escape his lips, and when his eyes return to the attic window, a man turns around and walks away.

'Richard!' he yells.

Art drops the pitchfork and hobbles back towards the house. Richard appears in front of him, but he walks through him.

'Arthur, you yelled for me?' Richard says. 'What is it?' He keeps to Art's pace.

'A woman… falling… hit the ground… Oh, the scream,' Art cries.

Richard glances down into the small courtyard. 'There is nothing there.'

Art looks over the fence, and there is no one there. He is about turn away when something catches his eye. Squinting, Art continues to stare, but without his glasses he's not sure what he has seen, so he hobbles down into the courtyard.

Art shuffles closer to the thing in the courtyard, bending down, and within seconds he turns away. He brings his hand to his mouth but too late; he vomits. As he makes his way back up the stairs, Richard's eyes widen at Art's demeanour.

'What is it?' he demands.

Art shakes his head as he places his trembling hand against his mouth. Richard wanders into the courtyard, but there is nothing on the concrete.

'Out with it!' he demands as he stands in front of Art.

'There was a small amount of blood, but if this is a memory, how can this be?' Art says.

Richard rubs his forehead, letting out a sigh. 'The only thing I can think of is that when you and the girls see images of the past, fragments of them may be left behind.'

'You're telling me the past can invade the present?' Art demands.

'I'm not sure, but with Henry causing trouble and me with no memory, maybe the memories are coming out.'

'Great, and now the girls will see things too. Richard, please remember so this can all stop,' Art begs.

'I want my memories back just as much as you,' Richard says.

Chapter 50

I open the shed door. Rays of light peer through the small doorway, highlighting the bogey. Footsteps run down the path towards me.

'Don't you dare sit on the bogey!' Lou yells.

Shaking my head, I roll my eyes. I grab the bogey, pulling it towards me, but it's stuck. I grab it with both hands and tug; it moves a little. Taking a deep breath, I tug at it again, but it won't budge. I put my foot on the bogey and pull, but I fall backwards and the shed is gone.

The sun is streaming through the trees as the leaves flutter in a gentle breeze. A giggle comes from behind me, so I turn around. A woman swings her arms around a man's neck and squeals.

'I love it. It is so beautiful; I'll never take it off,' she says, planting a kiss on his lips.

Her back is still facing me, but she stretches out her hands in front of her and tilts her head as she admires a ring. I tiptoe towards the couple.

'What?' I say, covering my mouth to stop any more words escaping my lips. The ring on her finger has diamonds and sapphires in a rectangle casing. *It's the same ring Mum had restored.*

The man's face isn't clear, but the woman turns around and her face is vivid. It's Ada, and she is bouncing up and down while admiring the ring. Her smile is radiant. I step backwards and I'm back in the garden. Lou is holding my hand.

'It's my turn; now give me the bogey,' she demands.

I tug on the rope, and Lou pulls back.

'I said it was my turn, so stop being mean!' she continues.

We glare at each other while pulling the rope in opposite directions. A gentle breeze brushes past while the sun still shines. I yank the rope and Lou steps forward, but she pulls back and I fall a few steps forward as I tug back.

'It's my turn!' I yell.

'No, mine!'

Glaring at her, I grind my teeth, and as I pull back, I let go of the rope. Lou falls backwards.

'Enjoy playing with it by yourself,' I snap.

She pulls the bogey towards her. 'Ooo, what's wrong with you?' Lou asks.

Narrowing my eyes, I snap, 'The ring Mum has—well, it was Ada's. I saw a man give it to her.'

'No, you didn't. You were standing with me by the shed the whole time,' Lou snaps.

'We both know this house is haunted. You've seen them.'

Tightening her hand around the rope, she stamps her feet. 'No, no, no. There are no ghosts,' she insists.

I raise my eyebrows and clench my jaw. 'Lou!' I shout.

Letting out a sigh, Lou groans and hunches her shoulders. 'Fine, there are ghosts. Just don't tell Mum I agree with you.'

Letting out a laugh, I say, 'I won't. Have you seen anything lately?'

Shaking her head, she says, 'Not lately.' Her eyes narrow and a few moments pass before she blunts out, 'Earlier, I saw a man step onto a table, and there was a rope hanging from the ceiling.'

Chapter 51

I pull Lou around the corner by the pear tree. She yanks her hand back, rubbing it with her other hand. Her eyes narrow while she taps her foot.

'What's with you and the pulling?' she asks.

Placing my hands on my hips, I scowl at her. 'I don't want Mum seeing us talk. Now tell me exactly what you saw!'

Out of the corner of my eye, I see the handle of the shed move. A loud bang comes from inside the door. Placing my finger over my lips, Lou copies me as we tiptoe towards the shed. I open the door carefully, and a can rolls out of the shed and to my feet.

Letting out a sigh, I turn back to Lou and say, 'Well?'

Lou shrugs her shoulders. 'What is there to say? I told you everything,'

I close my eyes tight, squeezing the bridge of my nose. 'Oh, come on Lou,' I snap at her. 'Did you see the man's face? Did he say anything? Was anyone with him?' I fire all these questions to her.

Leaning against the wall, Lou pauses for a moment, deep in thought, and then stares at me. 'I ran to the living room to put the telly on, but I saw a table in the middle of the room. A man with his back to me was crying. He stepped on a chair and grabbed the rope, and then he disappeared. I think he was on his own. Mum came in the room and asked if I wanted ice cream.'

'Weren't you scared?' I ask.

'At first, I was, but the nice ghost doesn't scare me anymore, and the mean one, I haven't seen him in ages.'

'Let me rectify that for you! Hello, Lou. Ann,' Henry says.

Lou and I turn our heads and stare at the shed door. The poltergeist leans against it with his arms folded, his bulging white eyes staring back at us. The air turns cold and the stench of death hits us both. Lou turns around and her body trembles as she throws up in the corner.

'Now, is that any way to great the mean one?' Henry gleams.

Lou grabs my hand as we step backwards. Not moving from his spot, Henry's smile widens.

'Stay and have a chat with me. Your conversation was very interesting,' Henry says.

'You were listening?' I ask.

He steps forward and picks a pear from the tree. It turns rotten in his icy hand, and when he bites into it, he savours the taste.

'Do you know, I planted this pear tree and the apple tree?' he says, pointing to them both in turn.

'Were you a servant here?' Lou asks.

Henry shakes his head. 'You are a naïve little thing, aren't you? I wasn't a servant here,' he hisses.

'Then how do you know Ada?' I ask.

Henry's hand clenches as his eyes narrow. 'Never mention that name to me again.' He steps closer, but takes a step back, adding, 'But… I do know who stepped onto the table with the rope.'

Lou and I glance at each other and then back at Henry. I let go of Lou's hand and take a step forward.

'Then who was the man?' I demand.

A smirk creeps across his face as he struts towards us. 'Wouldn't you like to know?' he says before disappearing.

Chapter 52

After Henry leaves, the warm rays of sun return and a light breeze touches my arms. Ignoring it, I turn around and kick the tree trunk.

'Why does he always talk in riddles?' I spit.

A sniffling sound breaks my train of thoughts. I turn towards the wall and glance down to find Lou crying.

'He scares me, Ann. He has no eyes and he smells,' Lou sniffles.

Her body trembles as she brings her hand up to wipe her tears away. I grab a tissue out of my skirt pocket and hand it to her. Lou takes it from me and uses it to wipe her face.

'Are you okay?' I ask.

'He just scares me,' she says, taking a few deep breaths. 'I wish he would go away and leave this house.'

'I think we can get rid of him if we help Richard remember,' I say.

Lou's smile returns and she disappears. I glance around and find I'm in the upstairs hallway of the house. It's dark and poorly lit. Footsteps race up the staircase while the screams get louder.

'Don't you dare walk away from me,' the man says.

The woman gets to the top step when her arm is pulled back, forcing her to turn around and face him.

'I can't talk to you when you're like this,' she begs.

His breathing becomes loud as he flexes his arms, towering over her. He gets close and jabs his finger in her cheek.

'You have betrayed me!' he yells.

Her lips and body tremble while her eyes dart from side to side. Her face is now clear—it's Ada. She reaches out to him, but he hits her arm away.

'I was lonely and you are never here,' Ada replies.

The man's face isn't clear, but his voice is deep and cruel as he hurls insults at her.

'My wife, the whore. All I can say is your standards have slipped, and you will pay for making me the laughing stock of the community,' he snarls.

He turns to walk away, but then he turns back to Ada with the full force of his hand. She grabs her cheek as tears stream down her face. He shoves her to the ground. She glances up; her hair falls loose around her face. She pushes a section back so she can meet his gaze. He smirks as he kicks her in the leg, grinding his teeth.

'You will pay for allowing another man to touch you and making a fool of me!' he yells, storming down the stairs and slamming a door.

She turns her head in my direction and stares for a moment, disappearing before me. My eyes dart around; I'm still in the hallway. However, the large window over the stairs lets the sun light peer through.

I freeze as the door downstairs opens. Footsteps stomp through the hallway and start to ascend the stairs towards me, making me shudder. Catching my breath, I tiptoe forward, peering over the banister to find Uncle Art coming up the stairs. I let out a sigh as a smile widens across my face.

'Why are you stomping, Uncle Art?' I ask.

'I always stomp when I have my boots on,' he says as he narrows his eyes. 'Are you alright, Ann?'

Shaking my head, I say, 'I saw Ada get pushed by her husband, I think, but I couldn't see his face. He told her she would pay. What does that mean?'

Uncle Art lets out a sigh once he finishes climbing the stairs. 'It means her husband wanted revenge.'

'She fell out of the window… Does that mean she was—'

'Pushed? I think it's possible.'

Chapter 53

Pacing around the garden, Richard is deep in thought. The memories he has regained still haven't told him about his death. He stops and glances around him, laying his eyes on the rosebush that Art's late wife used to grow. He strolls over and bends forward, clutching the base of the flower. Taking in a deep breath, he inhales the sweet scent of the rose, and when he lifts his head, the garden is different. Stepping back, he spins on the spot, and the small wall separating the lawn and the vegetable patch is gone. The lawn continues right through to the greenhouse.

Many people surround him and he sees himself serving drinks while laughter echoes around him. A clink of a glass silences the guests. A man is standing on the balcony with his glass raised; however, Richard can't make out his face.

'Thank you all for coming. It has been a busy period, and I'm pleased to say, the deal went through. Ed, couldn't have done it without you,' he says, raising his glass to Ed. 'Now, where is my beautiful wife?'

The man scours the crowd. 'There you are,' he beams, while gesturing her to come up to the balcony.

A woman makes her way up the steps and into the man's arms. It's the woman from the photograph, Ada. Richard notices himself narrow his eyes before offering more drinks.

'Now, would you please raise your glasses to my wife, as she has given me the best news,' says the man on the balcony. 'That is to say, my darling wife is pregnant, due in the autumn.'

The guests yell out congratulations as he plants a kiss on her cheek. Ada smiles to everyone while holding the man's hands. He helps her back down the stairs and approaches Richard, says something to him, and then he struts off back into the crowd with a grin on his face.

Now, the garden is empty and Richard is alone. Standing motionless for a moment, a pang of loss sweeps through him. As Richard ambles back towards the house, Art comes out to the balcony and calls after him, but Richard doesn't respond.

Art hobbles down the steps and comes close to Richard, calling his name once more. Richard glances up at Art and just stares at him without a word.

'What's happened? Did Henry attack you?' Art asks.

Shaking his head, he walks past Art and up the stairs. Art follows behind him, shouting, 'Richard, talk to me or I can't help you.'

Richard stops and turns around. He opens his mouth but closes it again. Art narrows his eyes and folds his arms, waiting for a response.

'Fine,' Richard spits. 'I saw myself serving people at a garden party here. Ada's husband had his arm around her, and I looked angry for a moment. Ada and her husband announced they were having a baby. Then the man came over to me and said something, and when he walked away, he looked smug.'

Art raises his eyebrow and says, 'Sounds like you were jealous of them because she picked him. My question is, why work for them when you liked her?'

'I don't remember courting her, I just remember her smiling at me outside the new theatre.'

'Maybe this is the start of your memories coming back,' Art says.

'If only I could remember who her husband was,' Richard says.

Chapter 54

A few months later, we visit my uncle again. I stroll into the living room, shivering. Uncle Art turns on the fire and places a cover over my shoulders. He does the same for Lou. The room is dark due to the grey clouds covering the sky. The wind whistles through the trees as it brushes against the thin window pane.

'It's bitter out there today,' Uncle Art says. 'I think it may snow soon if this keeps up.'

Lou gleams with excitement and says, 'Snowball fights, yay!'

I roll my eyes and then smile. 'I'd win, you know.'

'More like I'd win,' she retorts.

I poke my tongue out at her before turning my attention back to the telly.

We're sat there staring at the screen when footsteps come from behind us. Turning in unison, we see Uncle Art place mugs of hot chocolate on the side table and leave the room. Tossing our blankets to the floor, we each grab a mug and drink the contents. Moments later, we turn back around and find Henry standing in front of us, blocking the telly. Through his body, the dust particles float. He widens his stance and folds his arms, glaring at us. Lou crawls behind me, peering over my shoulder.

'What do you want?' I ask coldly.

'Weren't you told to respect your elders?' Henry snaps back.

I narrow my eyes at him while my body shakes. I snap, 'Yes, but you haven't been nice to me or Lou.

You took me to that horrible place and you play silly games.'

Henry snarls at me. The room grows colder and the stench becomes stronger.

Uncle Art walks in, shouting, 'What is all the yelling for?' He freezes to the spot when his eyes rest on Henry. 'Girls, come here, and you... get out!' he demands.

Lou crawls towards the chair, pulling herself up, and runs towards Uncle Art. I shuffle backwards and pull myself up using the side table. I rush towards Uncle Art, but Henry grabs my arms, dragging me back toward him. I yank my arm free and dart forward towards Uncle Art and Lou.

'Oh no you don't,' Henry snarls.

He grabs my arm once more as the stench of death surrounds me. Henry tightens his grip, holding me in place.

'The ring for your niece, old man,' he says.

Uncle Art's eyes widen, his grip on Lou tightening as she wriggles to free herself. He pulls her backwards towards him, staring at Henry. His eyes dart to me and then back to the poltergeist.

'Ann, are you okay?' he asks.

I nod, heaving from the stench radiating from Henry. I cover my mouth.

'Henry, please let her go. She is a child,' Uncle Art begs.

Henry doesn't respond, but as I look around the room, the walls turn blood red. The air grows colder, and as I open my mouth, a misty cloud escapes my lips. I flex my fingers, but it's getting even colder. I try to move, but Henry holds me in place. My body feels numb as the darkness creeps in and Uncle Art and Lou disappear.

Chapter 55

Alone in the darkness, I shut my eyes tight and open them again, but I'm still here with nothing around me. Henry isn't here. As rays of light break through the darkness, the large window in the hall stares back at me. The sun consumes the darkness. I'm now standing at the top of the stairs in the house, but the atmosphere is tense. A thud breaks the silence. Moments later, a cry echoes across the house.

Ada runs out of the bedroom, her clothes dishevelled and her dark brown hair dangling around her face. She glances back with tears in her eyes while her body trembles. A man storms out of the room and grabs her hair. She whimpers in pain as he pulls her back and seizes her by the throat. Ada's eyes widen as he squeezes. She groans and claws at his hands; he grins at her, baring his teeth. He lets her go and she drops to the floor.

She gasps for breath, supporting her body with her arms, and when she coughs, he grabs her by the back of the dress, dragging her back to her feet. Ada turns to face him; her body trembles while the colour drains from her face.

'Please, Henry—I beg you—' she cries as her voice breaks. 'I'm sorry, I will be a dutiful wife.'

The man's face becomes clear. His brown eyes darken with hatred as his chiselled cheekbones become even more prominent.

'Who do you love? Him or me?' Henry rages.

Her lips tremble as she stares into his eyes and, in that moment, his fist rises up into the air and catches the side of her face. A crunch echoes as her head turns away. Ada lets out a whimper as she brings her hand to her face.

'You love him, don't you?' Henry screams at her. 'You whore!'

She staggers to her feet and runs up the stairs to the attic. He glances in my direction, eyes bulging, and clicks his neck from side to side.

Ada was married to Henry, and now he is the poltergeist!

Following them into the attic, I tremble, my heart racing with every step. A sound from behind me grabs my attention, but when I glance back, nothing is there. Closing my eyes for a moment, I pray that I will be back with Uncle Art and Lou, but when I open them again, the attic rooms are in front of me. A gurgling sound comes from one of them. As I get closer the putrid odour is overpowering. I tiptoe around the door, and find Henry throwing blows, one after the other, at Ada while she tries to protect herself. Sweat is pouring down his face with each strike he makes.

'What do you have to say for yourself?' he demands.

Lowering her arms for a moment, her tearful eyes stare back up at him. 'I'm sorry—please stop,' Ada begs.

He drags her to her feet and spits in her face. For a moment, he breaks eye contact. Glaring back at her, a grin creeps across his face.

'You're right. I need to stop, my darling, and you need to rest.'

'Oh Henry, we can make a go of this, and I swear, I will devote my time to you and our son,' she cries.

Henry pulls Ada in, grabbing her around the waist, and bites her lip while kissing her. Ada flinches from the pain while tears roll down her cheeks. He edges forward, keeping a tight grip around her waist. Breaking the kiss, he strokes her cheek.

'Now, my darling wife, it is time to rest,' he sneers.

She smiles at him and is about to say something when Henry pushes her backwards. She stumbles; he grabs her legs, lifting her up, and pushes her out of the window. As her screams echo around the room, Henry holds open his hand; the ring is in his palm. He throws it across the room. When her body hits the courtyard below, an audible thud vibrates through the window. A scream comes from behind me. I turn around, and I'm back in the living room.

Chapter 56

Standing there in the living room again, opposite Lou and Uncle Art, sweat pours down my face while my body trembles. I clap my hands over my head to block out the echoing scream I can still hear. My heart races and a shudder sweeps through my body. I close my eyes tight and reopen them, but the images are still there. The bile in the back of my throat tries to escape, but I force it back down.

'Ann, what's wrong?' Uncle Art cries.

He's in his chair, looking up at me while holding both my hands. 'Ann, talk to me. What happened?'

I open my mouth, but no words come from my lips. I'm swallowing hard as I pause to gather my thoughts. 'Ada...' I stutter.

'What about Ada?'

My eyes dart around the room. Lou is sitting on the arm of the chair next to us.

'You saw something, didn't you?' she asks.

I nod in agreement. 'The window—Ada falls.' I gulp. 'It was Henry. The poltergeist.'

Uncle Art closes his eyes for a moment and pulls me in for a hug. 'It will be okay, Ann, I promise you,' he whispers.

'I heard another scream, but I don't know who it was,' I add.

Uncle Art strokes my hair and then pulls me out to face him. 'Did he show you what he did?'

'He wasn't there, so I don't know,' I murmur.

The air becomes cold and the walls turn blood red. Henry appears back in the room with his nostrils flaring. He storms over to us.

'Where did you go?' he explodes.

Uncle Art pulls Lou and me into his grip. 'You are not taking the girls. You killed Ada, didn't you?' he demands.

Henry's eyes narrow. He folds his arms. 'Did I? I don't remember. Either way, she deserved it.'

As my eyes dart back and forth between them, Uncle Art shakes his head. 'What did she ever do to deserve being thrown from a window?'

'I didn't say I did anything.' Henry smirks.

'I'll ask again. What did Ada do?' Uncle Art yells.

'She betrayed me.'

'How?'

'I have no time for your questions. Now give me Ann and get me the ring,' Henry demands.

Henry pulls on my arm while Uncle Art grips my waist even tighter. 'The girls are not pawns in your sick, twisted game, Henry. There will be no exchange,' he snaps back.

Henry raises his eyebrows and smirks. 'You underestimate me, old man.'

He grabs my arm and yanks me forward. Uncle Art pulls me towards him while I try to dig my heels into the carpet. However, Henry yanks again, and I fall into his grip.

'Told you, old man, you are no match for me,' he boasts. 'Now, I want that ring, and then you can have Ann back.' And we disappear into the darkness.

Chapter 57

Back in the darkness, Henry's grip is tight around my hand. I try to pry his fingers away, but his unnatural laugh echoes around me.

'You can keep trying, but you are here to stay until I have that ring,' he declares.

'Let go of me. I want to go home!' I demand.

His sinister snigger continues as his white eyes glare through the dark at me. 'Get comfortable because you're staying here.'

Tears stream down my face as the meaning of his words sinks in. I stumble backwards in hopes I will gain my freedom, but he keeps his grip on my hand.

'What will I eat or drink while I'm here?' I cry.

'You'll die of starvation. Let's hope your uncle comes to his senses before you do,' Henry hisses.

The whispers encase me while the tormented screams continue to get louder. Both my hands are free and I turn away from the sounds, but they follow me. My body is cold. I try to wrap my arms around myself to keep warm, but nothing works. My eyes dart around the bleak darkness, but there is no way out. I step forward; the sinister whispers in my ears continue to torment me. I turn around and start running in the opposite direction, but the screams only become more harrowing and depraved. Frozen to the spot, tears run down my cheeks as I sniffle, I look around in all directions but there is no light, just the darkness for company.

'Someone help me!' I scream.

There's a hardening in my stomach as my breathing becomes shallow. I clench my fist and then release. I gasp for breath while the tears burn my cheeks, their salty taste entering my mouth.

'Anybody, please help!' I cry.

No voice answers back. I sprint in a random direction, but the bleakness follows me. My lips quiver; my hands shake as I let out a whimper.

'I'm scared, please help,' I beg.

A whisper comes, too close to my ear. 'The longer you stay here, the more harm you will come to...'

'Then help me,' I plead.

'We can't get involved,' the whisper replies.

'What! Why?' I wail.

My head becomes light and a figure appears at the corner of my eyes. I turn, but nothing is there. My stomach is churning. I bring my hand to my mouth to stop the nausea, but it's too late. The pungent smell of vomit travels through my nose, but when I glance downwards the darkness hides it. I squeeze my eyes shut and open them again, but the dark is still here. Although the whispers and screams continue around me, no one answers my questions.

I clench my jaw; my hands keep moving as I start pacing. Sweat pours down my face even though I'm cold. A noise comes from behind me and I flinch. My heart races in my chest while my arms become itchy. I turn around, but nothing's there. An eerie laugh comes from another direction, and when I turn to face it, Henry is standing over me.

'Having fun?' he sneers.

'No, I want to go home now!' I demand.

'Once I have the ring then you can go, but until then, have fun.' He smirks before disappearing back into the darkness.

Chapter 58

Lou sits waiting for Uncle Art to come back. His voice bellows through the house as he calls out for Ann.

'Ann, where are you? Are you hurt?'

This he repeats as he goes from room to room. A sweet scent catches Lou's attention over the musty odour of the armchair. She turns her head in both directions but sees nothing. A few moments pass before Richard appears in the armchair to the side.

'What's wrong with your uncle?' he whispers.

Lou folds her knees into her chest and stares at him. 'The mad one took her, and Uncle Art is looking all over the house,' she cries.

'What happened, Louise?' Richard asks.

She glances down to her knees and doesn't speak. Richard edges forward, lowering his tone to almost a whisper. 'Lou, please look at me.'

Lou glances up, making eye contact.

'I need to know what happened so I can help your sister.'

Letting out a sigh, Lou straightens her legs and fidgets in the seat. 'He says he wants the ring and Ann will be with him until he gets it,' she whispers.

Richard's eyes widen. The air turns cold and putrid. Lou brings her knees back to her chest while her eyes dart around the room.

Richard stands up and yells, 'Henry, show yourself!'

Henry appears in front of him with a smirk across his face. The rancid smell of death lingers in the air, making Lou heave. Henry glances over at her and his grin widens.

'You bellowed, Richard?'

Richard glares at Henry as he steps closer and clenches his fist. 'Bring Ann back right now. She is a living person and won't last long on the other side,' he demands.

Folding his arms, Henry continues to stare at Richard while shaking his head. 'The ring for the girl. That is the deal.'

Richard's eyes narrow and his fist clenches even tighter when Henry disappears while letting out an eerie laugh.

Rubbing his face with both hands, Art storms into the living room and rushes over to Richard. 'Where's Ann?' he barks.

'I honestly don't know. I promise I will look, but I really don't know,' Richard whispers.

Rubbing his eye with his hand, Art continues to stare at Richard. 'Then go and find her... please,' he begs.

Richard glances at Art and Lou before disappearing to find Ann.

Lou tugs on Art's shirt, and he turns and looks down at her. Tears trickle down her cheeks. They stare at each other without saying a word before Art closes his eyes, pulling her in for a hug.

***

Taking a deep breath, Richard steps into the bleak darkness. A nauseating smell hits his nose, making him turn away. The agonised screams echo around him. Moments of silence are broken by supernatural whispers.

Richard glances around in the darkness and the torturing of souls is all that surrounds him. One curdling scream grabs his attention. Richard turns towards the ear-spitting sound, catching a glimpse of a torturer plucking the eyes from a soul's sockets while blood pours down their face. Richard turns away, forcing the bile back down his throat.

Further through the dark, another torturer is thrusting needles into a soul. Their eyes bulge while they struggle to become free. The torturer stops, tightens the straps, and then continues. Richard closes his eyes tight for a moment in order to regain his composure. Opening them again, he continues forward, searching for Ann in the darkness.

The indecipherable whispers continue in his ear as he walks on. He wants to call out, but if he does, it may alert Henry to his presence.

A whisper suddenly becomes clear. 'There isn't much time left.'

Richard catches a faint aroma through the fetid stench. He focusses on it and travels in its direction. As the aroma becomes stronger, an almost overpowering mixture of putrid smells, he allows a smile to form. When he gets to its strongest point, his hazel eyes dart around the darkness, but Ann isn't there.

Henry appears in front of Richard with a smirk across his face.

'Good luck finding her,' he gloats before fading into the dark once more.

Chapter 59

Richard goes back to the attic. Holding on to the windowsill, he looks to the floor and screams. A scraping sound from behind grabs his attention. He turns around and a table is in front of him. Glancing to the side, the bed is at an angle. The door is wide open, and when he looks up, he notices a rope hanging down.

He steps forward, and out of the shadows, his living self comes into view, uncharacteristically unkempt. As tears roll down his face, his chin starts to tremble. He sniffles and pulls out a handkerchief to blow his nose and wipe away the tears. When he catches sights of the initials *AR*, the living Richard's crying starts again. He pulls over a chair, steps onto it and then the table. As he sniffles, he places the rope around his neck.

Richard's eyes widen as he witnesses the memory playing out. He screams at himself to stop, but it carries on. He tries to knock the table over but falls through onto the wooden floor below. A voice comes from the doorway but it's muffled. A thud comes from above him, and when he gets up and turns around, the table is on its side and his lifeless body is swinging in mid-air. Turning to the doorway, he sees Henry leaning against the arch with a smirk across his face.

'Finally, you did the right thing,' he taunts, whistling as he walks away.

Richard turns to the window and back to the doorway, and now, the room is empty, apart from the picture of Ada on the windowsill. He takes a step towards it, when Art walks in the room.

'I thought you were looking for Ann?' Art enquires.

Richard glances at the floor and then meets Art's gaze. 'I did. I went to the darkness. The things that go on there, no one should have to witness. I thought I was close to getting Ann out of there, but Henry turns up and taunts me. He says, "Good luck finding her."'

Richard grabs the windowsill with his fists. Turning to face Art, he adds, 'In other words, he knows I will help you, so he is going to make this extremely difficult. Have you got the ring to give to him?'

Art rubs his face and hobbles forward. He clears his throat. 'You need to find her, because how am I going to explain this to her parents? As for the ring, it's not here. You told me not to give it to him. If you can't help her, surely you know a ghost or being that can?'

Rubbing his chin, Richard is considering his answer when a scream comes from downstairs. Art hobbles out of the attic room while Richard disappears to investigate. The rancid smell hits Richard as he enters the living room.

Lou is backing away from Henry as he steps closer. The walls turn a bloodier red the longer he stays in the room. Richard grabs her arm and disappears with her. He reappears with her at the top of the stairs as Art hobbles from the last step connecting the attic.

'What happened?' Art asks as Lou runs into his arms.

'Henry appeared and I think he was about to take Lou as well. Arthur, please, I implore you, call your niece and get the ring back before things get any worse,' Richard begs.

'What?' Art answers.

'I'm already dead, but the girls… think of them. Thank you for everything you have done, but it's time to give him what he wants.'

'Come out, come out, wherever you are,' Henry teases, his voice travelling up the stairs.

The pungent smell hits Art; he tightens his grip on Lou and nods at Richard. 'Take Lou and make sure she is safe,' Art insists.

Lou's eyes widen at her uncle, and she is about to say something when he interrupts her. 'Louise, please go with him. Hopefully it won't be for long.'

Chapter 60

Art turns around and finds Henry tapping his foot. Art jumps, taking a step back. Henry closes the gap between them, his eyes bulging, baring his yellow teeth.

'Do you have my ring?' he hisses.

Art takes a few more steps back, trembling. 'I'll be making a phone call to get you the ring.'

Henry folds his arms and tilts his head. 'Finally. I will be back once you have made that call.'

***

When the call connects, Art takes a deep breath.

'Lil, I need the ring I gave you back.' After a short pause, his tone becomes firmer. 'I know what I told you, but things have changed, and now I need the ring back. When you come to collect the girls, please have it with you.'

Once the call ends, Art hobbles to the chair in the window and rests his head in his hands. He stares out of the window, thinking about Ann, when a voice comes from behind. He turns around, and Richard is standing there with Lou.

'Is it safe for her to come back yet?' Richard asks.

Art shakes his head and glances at the floor. 'Henry will appear soon, asking about the phone call I just made.'

'I see, but I can't do this for long. I hope you understand?'

Art lifts his head for a moment, before staring back at the window in the kitchen. 'I understand. Just keep Lou safe. That's all I ask,' he whispers.

'I love you, Uncle Art,' Lou cries, breaking Richard's hold to hug her uncle. However, the moment is broken by the stench filling the air. Richard grabs Lou's arm and vanishes before Henry appears.

'So, old man, is the ring on its way?' Henry snarls.

Art glares at Henry while shaking in the chair. 'How do I know Ann is alive and unharmed?'

Henry raises his eyebrows while a smirk creeps across his face. 'You don't, old man. I guess you will have to trust my word instead,' he sneers.

Art stands up from the chair and steps closer to the poltergeist. He swallows hard to push the bile back down his throat; the stench is overpowering. 'Trust you! You are the evillest, most manipulative being I have ever met. How can I trust your word when you keep changing the rules?' he growls.

Henry's grin widens. 'Old man has a backbone? Interesting. I am a gentleman and when I give my word, I mean it. In other words, you can trust my word. If you had given the ring back in the first place then I would not have had to stoop to these measures.' Henry smirks. 'When you have the ring in your hand, call my name and I will bring your precious Ann and we will exchange items.'

Art's eyes narrow as his fist clenches. 'Ann is not an item. She is a person. Just because you messed up your life, why should more people suffer?' he shouts.

'I had a good life, a very fulfilling one if you must know, and as for your niece… an item, person, I don't really care. Just get me the ring.'

Chapter 61

Once Henry disappears, the stench fades, and moments later, Richard reappears with Lou. Art takes a deep breath, letting out a sigh.

'I take it he has gone?' Richard asks.

Art nods while hugging Lou. He whispers in her ear and she smiles. She runs to the cupboard on the far side of the kitchen and opens the drawer. Richard glances at her and, turning back to Art, asks, 'What is that about?'

'Lou is searching for sweets,' Art answers. 'Now, do you know if Ann is okay?'

Richard lets out a sigh while leaning against the window, folding his arms. 'He keeps moving her so I don't know how she is doing,' he whispers.

Arts eyes widen and he darts a glance at Lou. She is busy pulling the sweets out of the drawer. He smiles at her but she is busy, so he turns back to Richard.

'I see. If you hear anything…' he whispers.

'Then I will let you know.'

The scent of fresh cut grass floats past Richard's nose. He peers into next-door's garden, where the neighbour is cutting the lawn. He turns back to Art, but he's gone. He is back in the attic room.

Ada is in the doorway. Clasping her hands together, she says, 'Mary, my husband needs a drink, and you will need to start preparations for dinner this evening.'

'Yes, madam,' Mary, the maid, replies. She bows her head, disappearing out of the room.

Alone, Ada smiles at Richard as she steps into the compact room.

'It has been a while,' she sighs. 'I'm sorry about my mother's behaviour that night. How is your head?'

'My head is fine, thank you for asking. How is married life?' Richard asks.

Ada breaks eye contact, glancing at the doorway. 'Um, good. I'm well provided for,' she whispers.

'I wanted to get to know you better...' Richard says.

Gazing into his eyes once more, Ada informs him, 'Mr Harris, I may have smiled at you, but my mother was right, I was engaged. Now I am married, so if you are to work here, we need to be clear: nothing can happen, because we are from different classes.'

He edges closer, resting his hand on hers, 'I may be a servant but I have worked hard to build my reputation and am very well respected. When we met that night, neither you nor your mother could tell my background. So, why does it matter now? You can lie to yourself, but I see through the lie—'

'What lie would that be, Mr Harris?' Ada asks, pulling her hand away.

'Newly married women often say that they are provided for and they are in love. You did not mention love, so are you happy?'

Her eyes widen as she clasps her hands together. 'Yes, of course I am happy,' she squeaks.

Now, the memory is gone and Richard is back, facing Art.

'Richard, are you alright?' Art asks.

Richard stares back at Art. 'The day I started here, Ada came and spoke to me and I asked her if she was happy,' Richard discloses, running his hand over his face. 'I don't think she was, and that is why I stayed.'

Art raises his eyebrow. 'Great, you were in love with the boss's wife.'

Glancing at the floor, Richard whispers, 'It looks like it, doesn't it?'

Chapter 62

My teeth chatter while I rub my arms to keep warm. Flexing my fingers, my eyes tear up and then they start to close. My energy drains as I stand in the darkness. My bottom lip quivers but I can't cry. The monotonous whispers surrounding me keep going. I try to listen but they don't make sense.

The putrid odour of death is overpowering and the bile at the back of my throat stays there, waiting to escape. Something grabs my arm; I jump and step away but it doesn't let go. It is abrasive as it travels up towards my neck. My eyes widening, I flinch. I rub my arm to get it off, but it's slimy. I shake my arm back and forth in the air.

'Get off me!' I scream.

A whisper moans close to my ear. I scream again but no one answers back. It lets go of my arm but starts to climb up the other arm. I drag my fingers down my cheek as the torment continues. Then it stops for a few moments, before a thorny object slides down my arm, causing excruciating pain to tear through my body.

'Why are you doing this to me?' I cry.

Now the whisper becomes clear. 'If you are here then you must be punished.'

The bile escapes my mouth as I tremble. My pulse races while a pain starts in my chest. I clutch my throat as try to slow down my breathing.

'Wait, I'm a child. I'm eleven years old and I have done nothing bad,' I squeal. 'Except, I tease my sister, but that's it.'

I keep getting jabs, and each time the pain increases. The tears roll down my cheeks as I try to back away. A rancid smell comes close to me, but I can't identify what it is. My skin burns as the temperature increases; I try to shake my arm to get rid of the cause of my pain, but now my skin is on fire. I bolt away, but the pain gets worse.

'Someone please help! I'm not meant to be here. I'm a child,' I beg.

I spin, in the hopes of seeing a glimmer of light but there is only darkness here. My breathing is erratic as I continue to shake. Now, the burning sensation is in my leg. I bend over to brush the pain away, but I scald my palm.

'I'm begging you, please stop!' I shriek.

An eerie laugh comes out of the darkness. Henry is staring at me with a grin on his face.

'Having fun?' he teases.

I rush towards him and hit him with my fists. 'My arm and leg are on fire. I want to go home!' I howl.

He grabs my arms, tightening his grip. 'When I have the ring you can return home. As for the burning, it may stop when you leave,' Henry gloats.

'I've done nothing wrong to be burnt like this. Why?' I cry.

'My dear girl, anyone here in the darkness gets punished. It can't tell if you're good or bad.'

'You are the evil poltergeist! You hurt your wife!'

His white eyes widen as he growls at me. 'I don't know where you are getting your information from but that is not true. I loved my wife and I was distraught when she died. I got put here by mistake,' Henry snarls as he closes the gap between us. 'And I will do anything and trade anyone to get out of this evil place, as I'm innocent of what you are suggesting.'

Chapter 63

In the living room, Lou presses her stomach against the back of the sofa, waiting for Mum to arrive. The grey clouds outside darken the room. Art switches on the lamp then hobbles to the window. There is no sign of Lily, so he hobbles back to his armchair. Art and Richard are staring at each other in silence when there is a thunderous knock at the door.

'It's Mum!' Lou squeals, racing towards the door.

Richard stands up, but Art says, 'Old habits die hard, right? I'll get it.'

When Richard sits back down, the knocking replays in his mind. As it fades, it becomes more familiar.

Back when he served the house, his room was in the attic. After finishing for the day, he'd retire to his room.

As the candle flickers in the corner and he starts to read, there is a tap on the door. Marking the page, he answers the door to find Ada standing there with her hands clasped together.

'Can we talk?' she asks.

Blocking the entrance, he glares at her. 'Isn't this against the rules?'

Her eyes glaze over as she bows her head, looking at the floor. 'What I said earlier was out of line. Please may I come in?' she whispers.

Richard removes his hand and lets Ada in, closing the door behind her. He folds his arms as he leans against the door while crossing his one foot over the other. 'What do you have to say?' he demands. 'You shouldn't be up here.'

Ada sits on the chair in front of the desk, staring at Richard for a moment. Taking a deep breath, she whispers, 'I'm sorry. Please don't leave.'

'Apology accepted, but I'm still leaving,' Richard grumbles.

He grabs the door to open it, but Ada rushes to place her hand over his to stop him. 'Don't leave. Please,' she begs.

Richard smiles at her, lifting her chin to meet his gaze. He whispers, 'Why?'

Wrapping her hand around his, a smile creeps across her face. 'I lied before. When we met, I wasn't engaged, but it was happening…' Trailing off for a moment, she turns away from Richard. 'I was intrigued by you. You stood up to my mother—not even Henry has done that. On my wedding day, I kept thinking of you. Each day you work here, the more I think about you.'

Richard folds his arms, still gazing at her. 'You said we are from different classes.'

Putting her head into her hands, she cries, 'I know what I said, Richard, but please stay.'

He steps closer, placing his hands on her waist, and turns her around. Pulling her into an embrace, he smiles. 'I'll ask again: why should I stay?'

Giving Richard a yearning look, Ada blurts out, 'I want you to stay because I love you.'

Richard gazes at her for a moment, letting the words sink in as a glow creeps across her face. He should let go and leave, but those eyes and her smile keep his arms holding her. She lifts up her arms, wrapping them around his neck. He leans in and caresses her face, lingering for a moment before kissing her.

Many years later, here Richard is, a ghost in the same house he found love.

Chapter 64

Richard stares into the fireplace as he slumps in the armchair. A roaring sound from the hall breaks his thoughts. Turning in the chair, he listens as Art argues with Lily.

'I told you this house was haunted, but you chose to ignore that!' Art yells.

'How can you blame me?' Lily says.

Art hobbles away from Lily into the living room, and she follows him. She slams the door behind her, and Art glares at her. His nostrils flare while Lily folds her arms, tears running down her cheeks.

'Ann is my daughter and you say this is my fault. How?' she cries.

Art glances at the floor. Rubbing his jaw, he stares back at Lily. She bites her lip while rubbing her face.

Pacing the floor, she whispers, 'Where is my daughter?'

'I don't know, Lil. If I did, I would tell you,' Art answers.

Richard gets up from the chair and trudges towards the door. Lou tugs at Art's arm, and points at Richard.

'Richard, are you alright?' Lou asks.

He turns and gives half a smile, when Lily asks, 'Lou, who is Richard?'

'Um, he's the nice ghost. He has been trying to find Ann.'

Lily, raising her eyebrow, glances at Art and back to Lou. 'Are you seeing your imaginary friends again?' she asks.

Lou stomps her feet and folds her arms. 'Mum, Richard is a ghost and Henry the poltergeist has Ann. The ghosts are real,' she snaps.

A stench catches Lily's attention. 'What is that smell? Uncle Art, are you burning something, or worse?' she enquires.

Art's eyes widen while his muscles tense. Covering his face, he shakes his head.

'Uncle Art, are you alright?' Lily asks as she steps forward.

The pungent odour becomes stronger. Lily's eyes dart around the room as the walls turn from a light grey to a blood red. Her hazel eyes bulge as she steps back. Spinning around, she catches sight of her uncle and Lou huddling together. Art opens his hand and Lily takes it. Henry struts through the wall with a wide grin on his face.

Stuttering as she points to Henry, Lily screams, 'You have my daughter?'

Henry places his hand on his heart. 'Why, yes, I do have your daughter, Ann. You can finally see me.'

Lily nods as Henry comes closer to her. Baring his yellow teeth, his rotting breath makes Lily heave. Henry brushes his sleeves and then glares at Lily with an even wider grin.

'It is so delightful when people are scared of you,' Henry sneers, closing the gap between them. 'Now, my dear Lil—you don't mind if I call you Lil, do you?'

Lily shakes her head and lets him continue. 'The ring, I want it back.' He sneers as he holds out his icy hand.

Trembling, Lily fumbles in her pockets. Henry glares at her, crossing his arms. He tilts his head forward and starts tapping his foot. 'My dear girl, I'm not a very patient man. Now, where is it?' he screams.

'It must be in my bag,' Lily mumbles.

'Then go and get it,' he barks.

Lily dashes toward the hall, and Richard taps Henry on the shoulder. Turning around, Henry smirks at Richard.

'Mr Harris, I haven't got time for your games,' he mocks.

Richard glares back at Henry as his brow furrows. His hand clenches.

'Oh dear, Mr Harris is lost for words.'

Richard raises his fist and punches Henry, causing him to stumble backwards and through the floor.

Chapter 65

Art drags Lou towards the hallway as the atmosphere turns bleak. He turns to Richard just before leaving. Richard, devoid of any emotion, gestures with his hand for Art to leave; Art nods and hurries towards the front door with Lily and Lou.

A gust of wind rushes past them, slamming the front door shut. The walls run with rotting flesh. A crack of thunder hits the floor in front of them. Art pulls his nieces tight into his embrace.

'No one is going anywhere!' Henry roars.

Richard screams from the front room, 'They have nothing to do with this! You have to accept that Ada loved me and not you.'

Still circling around Art and the girls, Henry causes another crack of thunder, and when Lou jumps, his eerie laugh echoes around them.

Richard storms into the hall. He stands wide, folding his arms. 'Cut the theatrics, Henry. It's time we had a chat. Leave these people alone and give Ann back,' he demands.

Rushing towards Richard, Henry grabs him by his collar and throws him back into the door. Henry punches Richard in the stomach, who falls to his knees.

'How dare you tell me what to do,' Henry snarls. 'And as for Ada, she was my wife. You forgot your place. Now I'm going to get my ring back.'

Turning his head back to Art, his white eyes gleam as his nostrils flare. Cracking his head from side to side, his grin widens as he creeps forward. 'Now give me the ring or else!' he demands.

Lou hides behind Art and her mum. The cracks of thunder continue as Henry rages. He pokes Art with his icy finger as Art moves his head backward.

'I told you, old man,' he growls, 'I will get what I want and you can't win.'

Out of the corner of his eye, Art catches Richard stumbling to his feet. Turning his attention back to the poltergeist, he gulps and Henry smirks.

'Lil... the ring... now!' Art demands.

Lily fumbles in her bag and pulls out a box. Her hand shakes as she places it into her uncle's hand. Art grips it tight, straightening his hand out in front of him. He opens his mouth, letting out a whimper while his body trembles. Henry, seething, tries to open Art's hand, but his fingers are stiff.

'Open your hand, old man, or you will die!' Henry bellows.

Art's hand shakes as each finger loosens its grip from around the box. Henry smirks, his white, bulging eyes gleaming. Tapping his fingers together, he waits for the moment in which he can snatch the box from Art's fingers and release himself from the bonds of darkness.

Richard lunges at Art and, as he lifts his third finger, grabs the box, disappearing through the door. Henry growls and chases after Richard, leaving Art and his nieces shaking. The bright yellow hall returns while the ghosts' voices fade into the distance.

An ear-splitting thud echoes through the house. Clutching onto each other, their eyes dart around, looking for the source, when a sharp scream grabs their attention. Lou tiptoes forward, but Art holds her back when footsteps approach, sprinting down the stairs.

Chapter 66

Henry rushes at Richard, but he ducks and flies out into the road while the cars whiz by. Darting up the street, Richard gains speed as Henry dashes towards him.

'Give me the ring!' Henry demands.

Glancing over his shoulder, Richard sees Henry is gaining on him. He sprints, increasing his speed. Turning right, Richard goes through the wall of a neighbouring house. He travels through each wall until he is back in number 13. Rushing up the stairs, he heads to the attic.

While waiting for Henry, he opens the box and discovers there is no ring inside. His eyes widen, his body frozen to the spot. Shaking his head, he stumbles backwards.

Still staring at the box, he squeals, 'No—where is the ring?'

He tips the box upside down but nothing falls out. Shaking it, only the velvet tray falls to the floor.

He turns to the picture of Ada. 'Did you somehow take the ring back? If you did, please send a sign,' he begs.

The almighty thud of the front door hitting the wall grabs Richard's attention. He bends down, grabs the velvet tray and rushes to place it back into the box. Snapping the lid shut, he places it in the small of his back. The racket of Henry dashing up the stairs makes Richard jump, but he closes his eyes for a moment and stands there in wait.

When he opens his eyes, Henry is seething as he creeps forward. He flexes his fingers while a smirk creeps across his face. The walls turn to rotting flesh as the odour of death fills the air. Stopping in front of Richard, he clenches his jaw and growls.

'Give me the ring and I won't kill you,' Henry spits.

'I'm dead already, so isn't that an empty threat?' Richard seethes.

Narrowing his eyes, Henry folds his arms while his posture stiffens. 'Are you sure it's an empty threat, Richard? I could send you to the darkness.'

'How can that be any worse than this?'

'Have you ever been to the darkness? No? Then let me enlighten you. The things they do there, the things you'll see, you can't possibly fathom.'

'If you were down there, then tell me how you got out. I mean, you want the ring.' Richard holds the box in front of him.

'A group of children found the ring and summoned me back. Pity they didn't know what they were doing, but oh well.'

'What did you do to get into the darkness?'

Henry comes right into Richard's face and growls. 'If you had behaved then I wouldn't have had to take care of things.'

The stench of his breath is overpowering, and Richard covers his mouth with his hand. Henry starts to stroll away, but the putrid scent still lingers in the air. Richard removes his hand, taking a deep breath, and rushes forward, grabbing Henry's arm.

'No more riddles. What did you do?' he yells.

Shrugging off his grip, Henry smirks at Richard and grabs the box. 'Thanks for the ring.'

'What about Ann?'

'What about her? I have no use for her now.'

'Then return her,' Richard pleads.

Henry lets out a laugh, his eyes gleaming. 'I'd love to, but she's dead,' he says, and disappears.

Chapter 67

I run into the living room but it's empty. I turn around, heading back to the doorway. Whispers become audible. My body trembles the closer I get to the hall. Taking a deep breath, clenching my fist, I tiptoe into the hallway. As I turn towards the front door, Lou pokes her head out. Tears roll down my face.

'I'm so pleased to see you, Lou,' I cry.

I stumble, but Mum and Uncle Art come from around the corner and catch me. Taking me into the living room, they place me on the sofa. Dust particles float above my eyes as the sun streams through the window. They start firing questions at me, my eyes darting between them.

'Stop!' I shout. 'Sorry, but you're going too fast. Please let me answer one question before you ask the next one.'

Uncle Art tilts his head, keeping his eyes firmly on me. Leaning in, he asks, 'What happened?'

I lower my gaze while I fidget with my hands. 'The poltergeist took me to this really horrible place. It was dark and I couldn't see anything or anyone. However, I could hear muffled sounds. Sometimes, though, there were piercing screams. It was so frightening. He even left me alone there.'

Placing his hand over mine, Art squeezes my hand and asks, 'Are you okay now?'

Shaking my head, I reply, 'Not really. I'm just glad to be back here.'

'How did you get out of there?' Uncle Art asks.

Glancing out of the window, I let out a sigh and turn back to Uncle Art. 'I screamed and screamed for help, but I was ignored. The longer I was there, it felt like I was not gonna—'

'Don't you mean, "going to"?' Mum interrupts me.

I tip my head forward and glance at Mum. Uncle Art glares at her. 'I hardly think this is the time to correct grammar, do you?' He looks at me and smiles. 'Please carry on, Ann.'

'Not going to make it,' I say, glancing at Mum. 'When suddenly something grabbed my arm and dragged me into the light. I didn't see who it was, but they whispered in my ear, saying I would be okay. Then, when I looked around, I was back in the attic, so I came running down the stairs.'

Mum sits at the end of the sofa, staring at me. She raises her eyebrow while pinching her chin, giving me half a smile. 'I know you believe in these stories, in this fanciful world of yours, but I think you've spent way too much time in this house. So, I think it's best we go home.'

I jump when Uncle Art yells. I turn my head to him, and he is glaring at Mum. His nostrils flare and his eyes narrow. 'Lil, this is no joke, and this is not a fanciful world of make-believe that Ann is making up. I don't know why you insist on thinking this is not real, but unfortunately it is.'

'This is an old house and the weird things that are happening in here must be down to a door or a window being open,' Mum says.

Uncle Art scoffs at mum. 'Okay, the wind howling through the house, that is a plausible explanation, but explain the walls changing colour. How is that done?'

Mum pauses and her mouth is open but no words come out. She rubs her forehead, staring at each of us in turn.

'Well?' Uncle Art demands.

'I haven't worked that one out yet,' she whispers.

'It doesn't matter now, as the poltergeist has the ring back, and with any luck, he will leave us alone,' Uncle Art says, getting up from the sofa and leaving the room.

Mum turns away and stares out of the window, placing her hand in her right pocket. I shake my head when she puts her finger to her lips. Closing my eyes for a moment, I rub my forehead. I open my eyes and glance at my lap.

'You still have the ring, don't you?' I ask.

Mum looks at me, glancing at the floor. 'It's a beautiful ring, and your uncle gave it to me. I paid to have it repaired, and now he wants it back to give it to some poltergeist that you all seem to believe exists.'

'This is no joke, Mum,' Lou interjects. 'That mean poltergeist is real, and he wants the ring, so you should give it to him.'

Mum sits on the sofa, and the dust particles float in the sunbeams coming through the window. She lets out a sigh and grabs Lou's hands, pulling Lou towards her.

'I wish you could understand, but a ghost or a poltergeist—if they are real—will not need such things as jewellery'

Lou yanks her hands away and stomps her feet. 'They are real, and this is no joke,' she insists.

'Mum, Lou is right. These ghosts are real, and the poltergeist is very mean, and he will do anything to get that ring. He took me to such a horrible place. So please believe us,' I beg.

Mum stares at us both and lets out a sigh. 'Hmmm…' She clears her throat. 'It had to be a nightmare, right?'

Lou and I shake our heads. Mum closes her eyes while she pinches the bridge of her nose.

'Uncle Art is not going to be happy when he discovers I took the ring out of the box,' she says. 'I still have the ring.'

Chapter 68

A faint aroma of sulphur hangs in the air. I lift my nose and breathe it more deeply. It becomes stronger and fills the room. I smile when Richard enters the room with a smile on his face.

'I'm so glad you are alright, Ann. He didn't hurt you, did he?' he asks.

'No, but it was scary in the dark,' I say.

Out of the corner of my eye, I catch my mum's mouth opening, her eyes wide as she freezes to the spot. She rubs her eyes and stumbles closer.

'You're a ghost?' she asks.

Richard turns to her and nods his head. 'Yes, Lily, I am a ghost.'

'I... I saw you in the garden and spoke to you. I thought you were a friend of my uncle's. Not a ghost!' she stutters.

'If I had said I was dead, would you have believed me?'

'Umm, I guess not.'

'You've been speaking to Richard?' Lou and I ask.

Mum's eyes dart to us as she runs her hands through her hair while collapsing onto the sofa.

'It was months ago I saw him, but I didn't think he was a ghost. It's not possible,' she insists.

I roll my eyes as I look at Richard.

He smiles at me and says, 'Henry now thinks he has the ring.'

I look at Mum and then back at Richard. He turns to Mum and edges closer to her. Rubbing the back of his neck, he clears his throat.

'Where is the ring?' he asks.

Mum shifts a little while she rubs her nose, her bottom lip quivering.

'It's a gorgeous ring and I want to keep it,' she cries.

Shaking his head while he rubs his forehead, Richard glares at Mum. 'Do you have any idea what Henry is like? He has done questionable things. Evil things. For goodness' sake, he took your daughter to the dark place, and for a living human being that is not right.'

'But—'

Richard's eyes widen, and Mum shuts up as he bows his head a little. 'I haven't finished yet,' he says as Uncle Art hobbles back into the room. 'Your daughter was scared out of her mind, and the longer she was there, the worse it would be. Death would have been waiting to claim her as it cannot distinguish the living from the dead. But no, you go ahead, you keep the damn ring and let everyone else suffer. Make no mistake, Lily, this poltergeist named Henry will find you, and when he does, he will torture you until you give up the ring.'

Mum stares at the floor. 'I'm sorry,' she cries, putting her hand into her pocket and removing the ring. She holds out her hand and opens up her palm. 'Here is the ring.'

Uncle Art clears his throat, and Mum turns to face him.

'I thought you knew better than that,' he says.

'I really am sorry,' Mum says.

Uncle Art opens his mouth to speak, but the walls turn dark with blood trickling down. The stench of rotting flesh becomes more pungent. Lou and I huddle together on the sofa as the room grows darker.

'What's happening?' Mum screams.

Uncle Art hobbles toward us and shouts, 'Henry has discovered he doesn't have the ring, so he is on the way. This is how he makes his grand entrance!'

Mum runs to us and pulls us in tight. Her body trembles, her teeth chattering as the icy air grows colder.

Chapter 69

The room is now dark, and above us a thunderous crack sounds. A lightning bolt hits the floor in front of me. Lou and I jump and squeeze each other tight. Henry appears, his eyes wide and his fists clenched. His nostrils flare as he cracks his neck. The veins in his neck pulsate as he barrels towards me. I try to scramble away, but he grabs me, pulling me towards him. His breath reeks with a putrid stench. I try to hold my breath, but his smell still creeps up my nose and turns my stomach.

'How did you get out of the darkness? And give me my ring!' he snarls.

Blood trickles from the whites of his eyes as we stare at each other. My body freezes as I try to pull away. I try to turn away from him but he forces my head back so I'm still staring into his eyes. I force my eyes downwards.

'Look at me when I ask you a question. You really are a rude child!' he screams.

'What... I—'

'Answer the question. How did you get out, and where is my ring?'

'I got dragged to the light,' I mutter as my eyes dart around the room. 'I... I don't have the ring.'

'Don't lie to me about the ring. Who took you to the light?' Henry demands.

'I don't know who took me to the light; I didn't see their face. How could I have the ring when I was with you in the darkness?'

Henry glares at me, pausing for a moment. His eyes dart around the room. He lets go of my arm and I fall to the floor. He storms over to Uncle Art and shoves him into the wall.

'You're next,' Henry states as his grin widens. 'So, old man, where is my ring? And, just before you answer, I would advise you to think very carefully.'

Uncle Art's face turns pale while his body trembles. His eyes dart to me and then Lou and back at Henry. 'I… I don't have your ring,' he stutters.

Henry's whole body shakes as the veins strain below his transparent skin. He grabs Uncle Art and slams him against the wall, repeating his question.

'I don't have your ring!' Uncle Art repeats.

Henry tilts his head to one side and his eyes narrow. 'I'm not sure if you are lying, old man, but if you are, let me reassure you I will kill you!'

'I'm not lying,' Uncle Art states.

Henry turns from Uncle Art and grins when he spots Lou. Strutting over to her, he grabs her arm. Lou screams as she struggles to get away. I try and help, but Henry knocks me to the floor. Lou trembles, tears running down her cheeks.

'Get off me,' she cries.

I pull myself up and push Henry, but he doesn't move. He turns, glaring at me, and laughs.

'Better luck next time,' he gloats.

Uncle Art grabs Lou's other arm and pulls, but can't get her free. Henry's eerie laugh fills the air. He grabs Lou tight around the chest with one icy hand and holds out the other. Lou shakes her head, her lip trembling as she blubbers.

'Give me the ring and Louise will not be harmed,' Henry demands. 'It's your choice.'

'Mum, give him the ring,' Lou blurts out.

Now, Henry glares at Mum. Her eyes bulge the more he glares at her.

'So, you can see me. Good. Now, the ring please,' he repeats.

Mum's eyes dart to us and then to Uncle Art while her body trembles.

'Give him that damn ring, Lil,' Uncle Art insists.

Mum covers her face for a moment and then removes her hands. Henry stands tall in front of her with his arms folded, tapping his foot.

'I'm growing impatient,' he declares.

She pats down her pockets of her floral dress for the ring. Nothing. She puts her hands inside the pockets and fumbles around. Her eyes widen as she looks around the floor. When she lifts her head, Henry comes right into her face with a growl.

'Where is it?'

'It was in my pocket, but now it's not there,' she cries.

Chapter 70

Richard turns away as Henry grabs Lily by the throat and slams her into the wall. He glances at Lily as she gasps for breath. Her gurgles vibrate around the room, and he turns away. Closing his eyes, he tries to block out the sounds, putting his hands over his ears.

When he opens his eyes, the room has now changed, but the gurgles still echo. Turning around, he sees Henry has Ada pinned against the wall as she scratches with her nails to free his grip. The door swings open, and Richard storms in. Grabbing Henry by the collar and trousers, he throws him into the hall.

'You do not lay a hand on Mrs Roberts,' Richard growls.

Henry turns his head while pulling himself up to his feet. His eyes narrow and his nostrils flare as he stumbles back into the room while rolling up his sleeves.

'My house, my wife, my rules,' Henry seethes, as he shoves Richard. 'She took a vow to obey her husband and therefore is my property to do with as I see fit.'

'You are a coward,' Richard snaps back. 'Real men do not use their wives as a punching bag. This has got to stop.'

Ada's eyes dart between the men as she staggers towards the living room door. Henry catches sight of her moving and grabs her arm, pulling her towards him. His wide eyes narrow as her face comes close to him.

'You are not excused. I'm not done with you yet,' Henry hisses.

Richard lunges at Henry. Henry turns to him with a grin and punches him with his free hand. Richard stumbles backwards, knocking his head on a chair. As his eyes close, an audible rip of material echoes in his ears, followed by a scream.

Now, Richard opens his eyes and turns back around to see Henry laughing while the girls scream. Art is on the floor, staring at Richard and darting his eyes to Henry and Lily. Richard frowns while Art darts his eyes again. This time, Richard follows his gaze, and by Henry's transparent foot is the ring. Nodding at Art, Richard lunges at Henry, scooping up the ring while knocking Henry to the floor. Lily slides down the wall, holding her throat as she coughs, trying to regain her breath.

'Get off me,' Henry snarls.

'This is no longer your house, so show some respect,' Richard barks.

Lily crawls over to the girls and pulls them away. Their eyes dart away as Richard punches Henry. Henry's eyes narrow as a smirk creeps across his face. He raises his hands and grips Richard's neck, throwing him to the floor. Now on top of Richard, he bares his teeth.

'My house, my rules,' he snarls. 'But I think we have had this conversation before.'

Henry squeezes his grip while Richard hits the side of his arm. Henry's white eyes bulge, and he slaps Richard across the face.

'Stop interfering, it's none of your business. You are a nobody, Mr Harris.'

Loosening Henry's grip, Richard knocks him off. Stumbling to his feet, he spits, 'I'm not a nobody, Mr Roberts. Stop hurting this family and leave them alone.'

'Never!' Henry cackles.

Chapter 71

A knock at the door makes me jump. Henry's eyes burn into mine as he stares at me.

'Ann, you answer the door, and don't try anything,' he demands.

'Fine! Just remember, not everyone believes in or can see ghosts.'

I force myself to stand, stumbling a few steps before I run to the door. When I open it, the milkman is standing there.

'Hi, is your granddad there?' he asks.

Frowning, I scratch my cheek. 'Um, I think you mean my uncle. I think he's busy.'

His brows draw together as he tilts his head. 'I need to speak to him about his milk bill,' he insists.

I glance behind me while holding the door. 'Um...'

'I'm growing impatient, Ann,' Henry barks, from where he hovers inside the wall. 'Now get rid of him.'

'Are you okay?' the milkman asks.

I glance down for a moment and then stare back at him. He gestures with his finger for me to come closer. I hesitate but then I step forward. He bends down and whispers in my ear, 'I know about the poltergeist, and I heard what he said to you.'

My eyes widen as I pull away.

He smiles and nods. 'Tell your uncle that I'll visit a few more customers and I will be back in about an hour.'

'Okay, I'll tell my uncle.'

Shutting the door, I turn around. Henry is standing there, glaring at me.

'What did the milkman whisper to you?' he asks.

I rub the back of my neck as I shake my head. 'He said I could trust him as he knows Uncle Art. Can't someone be nice?' I lie, storming off into the living room.

Henry's eyes scan the room, narrowing. Foam starts to appear from his mouth as he creeps towards us. The room is dark and cracks of thunder surround us again. As the lightning strikes, the closer he gets.

'Where is Mr Harris?' he roars.

Uncle Art's face turns pale as he trembles, and he tries to avoid eye contact.

'He left the moment you followed Ann,' he stutters.

Henry's eyes widen, revealing more of the whites. He storms towards Uncle Art, baring his yellow teeth. The putrid odour becomes viler than before. Closing the gap between them, Henry presses his forehead against Uncle Art's.

'Where did he go?' Henry bellows.

'He just said he couldn't be around you, and then he left,' Art stutters.

Henry lets out a roar, picking up the side table and throwing it across the room, before storming out to find Richard.

Chapter 72

The rumble of Henry's rage vibrates through the house. Richard stares out the window as the noise becomes louder the closer Henry gets to the attic.

'Mr Harris, where are you?' Henry screeches.

Richard turns around, staring at the doorway for a moment before disappearing through the wall. When Henry storms into the attic room and discovers it is empty, he lets out a gut-wrenching roar. Spit forms in the corners of his mouth while his eyes bulge. The veins in his neck throb as he clenches his fist, punching the wall.

'Richard, come here right now. It is not a request but an order,' he demands.

Nothing but silence surrounds Henry. Letting out a roar, he storms through the wall into the other attic room but also finds it empty. The slamming of a door grabs Henry's attention.

Sprinting out of the room, he yells, 'I did not give you permission to leave my house!'

He charges towards the front door, but a loud noise from upstairs makes him turn around. Darting back up the stairs, Henry calls out to Richard.

'I just want to talk. Come on, Richard—you know it will be a friendly chat.'

Nothing. No response. Henry's body trembles. Clenching his fist, he punches the banister, kicking the step leading to the attic. Stalking up the stairs, Henry tilts his head, listening for anything that would tell him where Richard is. As he creeps further up the steps, thunderous cracks follow him. He glares up towards them.

'Go away and leave me alone,' he demands.

A loud noise comes from the room directly in front of him, Henry's grin widens as he creeps up the stairs. The metallic taste of the blood dripping into his mouth intoxicates him as he gets closer to the room. A whiff of success brings a glow to Henry.

'We have so much catching up to do, Richard. I hope you are ready.'

Pushing the door, Henry peeps around the corner. Against the wall near the window are stacks of furniture with a musty odour.

'Richard, come out of the shadows. I only want to talk.'

Nothing. Henry grinds his teeth, his nostrils flaring. Grabbing an armchair, Henry throws it across the room.

'I demand you show yourself!'

The walls turn dark with rotting flesh as the lightning lashes against them. A fetid decay fills the air as more furniture is thrown across the room. Henry cracks his neck, the veins straining against his transparent skin, and barrels towards the wall, rushing through into the next room. The bright walls turn to rotting flesh while the putrid odour follows him.

The photo of Ada sits on the windowsill.

'You whore!' he screams as he knocks it to the floor.

A gust of wind hits Henry off balance and he stumbles to the floor. Richard stands in front of Henry, glaring at him.

'How dare you knock the picture of Ada over.'

'So touching—you still care,' Henry growls, getting to his feet.

'Looking for this?' Richard holds out his hand.

The ring gleams as Henry stares at it. 'My ring!'

Henry goes to grab it, but Richard closes his hand. Wide-eyed, he glares at Henry.

'You want the ring, then come and get it.'

Chapter 73

Uncle Art shouts after me, but I ignore his pleas to come back. I run back towards the house and the dark cloud forming around it. My body trembles more the closer I get, but I ignore the hair rising on the back of my neck and my hardening stomach. I turn into the gate when a hand on my shoulder stops me. Turning around, the milkman smiles at me.

'It's time to leave them alone.'

Shrugging off his hand, I narrow my eyes. Taking a step back, I ask, 'Why? And how do you know about them?'

His smile disappears while his eyes flicker away. 'It's complicated.'

Folding my arms, I tap my foot. 'Did you live here, and is that why you know about them?'

The rain lashes down and I'm getting wet, but I stay and glare at him. Henry is barking at Richard, and the howling wind almost knocks me back, but I lean against the wall to stop the fall.

'I never lived here, but I know a family member that did. I thought they were joking at first until I started visiting the house, twenty years ago,' he says. 'Look, let's go back to your uncle and away from the house.'

I stroll with him towards Mum, Lou and Uncle Art as he explains. 'My family member lived here when they were a child, and then they moved away. Years later, they became suspicious when they got a letter so they started to dig deeper.'

I stop and stare at him, raising my eyebrow as I shake my head.

'Please don't look at me like that,' he says. 'I really can't say too much at the moment but I am telling the truth.'

'Really! Then how many ghosts are there?' I ask.

He hesitates for a moment as he glances around. Turning back to me, he says, 'There are two ghosts. However, one is a poltergeist, named Henry, and as I told you earlier, I heard what he said to you. I'm not sure the name of the other one. I asked, but my family member always avoided the question.'

'The ghost's name is Richard; he's the nice one.'

He opens his mouth, but Mum scoops me up in her arms, changing the subject. 'Why did you go back to the house?' she asks.

'Richard needs help,' I answer.

Letting go of me, Mum puts her head in her hand. 'No, no, no!' she repeats. 'Ann, Richard is dead—he will be fine, but you won't be. Henry has the ring, now let them fight it out!'

'Can I ask what ring?' the milkman asks.

Uncle Art glances at him for a moment and raises his eyebrow.

'I know about the ghosts; that's why I would never come in. I never want to meet Henry.'

'Rich, how do you know about Henry?' Uncle Art asks.

'It's complicated.'

'Never mind complicated, Rich—if you know something then it's time to let us know,' Uncle Art insists.

Rich rubs the back of his neck and his eyes dart away.

'Rich, I'm waiting!' Uncle Art shouts.

Chapter 74

Richard's eyes widen as Henry's grip tightens around his neck. A grin creeps across Henry's face as Richard tries to loosen his fingers.

'I remember the same look she gave me when I used to do this to her,' Henry says.

Then, Richard finds himself standing in the doorway of his room. Ada is clawing at Henry's fingers as she sputters. Richard runs up to them and drags Henry off her.

'What are you doing?' Richard snaps.

Henry pokes Richard in the chest. 'Since she loves being up here and involving herself with people below her station, I thought I would see what all the fuss is about,' Henry says, stumbling. 'I have to say, it is a kick. I can see why she comes up here often.'

Gazing at Ada, Richard notices her dress is torn, revealing most of her slender figure. Tears streaming down her face, Ada drags a sheet from the bed, covering herself.

Glaring back at Henry, Richard clenches his fist, but Ada lets out a whimper. He looks back at her, and she shakes her head.

Gritting his teeth while taking a deep breath, he yells, 'Mr Roberts, you are drunk. I think you need to sleep it off.'

Wrapping a hand around Richard's neck, Henry sneers, 'She's damaged goods now. I've had one last go at her in this…' he says as he glances around the room.

Turning back to Richard, he slurs, 'Keep her. She's not that good anyway.' Looking to his wife, he adds, 'You will never see our son again; I will make sure of that.' Henry glares at Richard, his eyes roaming up and down. Glaring back at Ada, he stumbles closer to her. 'I hope losing our son was worth it, because he's not got it where it counts.'

Richard grabs Henry by the scruff of his jacket, forcing him out of the room. After a few minutes, he comes back to find Ada shaking on his bed. He puts a towel around her, holding her close.

'I need to tell you something, Richard,' Ada whispers.

'Sssh, my love. No explanation necessary,' Richard answers, kissing her forehead.

And here he is again, all these years later, having a fight with Henry over Ada. The lightning strikes the floor in front of him and the pungent stench of rotting flesh turns his stomach even worse the more erratic Henry becomes.

'Remember everything yet?' Henry spits.

'Enough to know you were cruel to Ada and didn't deserve her,' Richard growls, taking another swing at Henry. 'Why could you never let her be happy?'

Smirking, Henry laughs at Richard as he circles him. 'She was my wife not yours. She disobeyed me, and you… you disrespected me and the position I gave you within my house. You turned her into a whore!'

Richard throws a punch, but Henry sidesteps. His eerie laugh fills the room as it grows darker. Striding towards Richard, Henry pushes him with both hands, knocking him to the floor.

He bends down, hovering over him. 'I will have my revenge, but first give me the ring,' he demands, holding out his hand.

Richard ignores his request, glaring at him.

Henry digs his knee further into his chest while baring his teeth. 'I will make things very unpleasant for you!'

'How is that possible, when we are both already dead?' Richard asks.

'I can take you to the dark side and keep you there long enough that they torture you.' Henry smirks.

Richard scrambles to get free, but Henry grabs his jacket, dragging him through the attic window to the courtyard below, where the darkness waits to welcome them.

Chapter 75

I start to run back towards the house. Lou screams at me to slow down so she can catch up, while Mum and Uncle Art chase us. Glancing over my shoulder, Mum is ahead of Uncle Art. In the distance, the milk float turns into the next street.

'Stop, right now!' Mum yells.

'Richard needs our help!' I shout back.

When Lou and I reach the house, a piercing scream echoes around us. The sky grows dark and the rain lashes down. Gripping Lou's hand, I trek up the steps to the red door. The wind howls as lightning strikes.

'It will be okay, right?' Lou asks.

I stare at her while I bite my lip. 'Maybe,' I say. 'You don't have to come, Lou. Things might get weird.'

Lou takes a deep breath. 'I want to,' she answers.

Holding the brass knob, I push, and the creaking door echoes through the hallway. The eerie silence makes me stop in the doorway. I gulp down my breath. *Is Henry waiting around the corner?*

Lou tightens her grip around my hand, slapping her other hand over her mouth to silence her whimpers as tears roll down her cheeks. We glance at each other once more and step forward. The door slams shut behind us and I jump. Turning my head, no one is there.

The jaundice yellow walls trickle with blood as we trek forward. A piercing scream echoes through the hallway. Lou breaks free of my hand and darts for the front door, but it's locked shut. She turns to me and her lip quivers.

'I want to leave,' she cries.

'You had your chance, and now we are stuck here. Come on.'

I hold out my hand, and she wraps her small hand in mine. I take a deep breath and step forward. Writing appears on the wall.

Get out, while you still can.

Closing my eyes tight, I wait for a few seconds and open them again, but the writing is still there. Lou is crying; I turn to her, and she trembles as she gasps.

'I tried to get out, but we're stuck,' she cries. 'What are we going to do, Ann?'

'Keep thinking that we'll be okay.'

When we turn the corner, the hallway is dark, and as I glance through the door to the kitchen, it's now a dining room. I glance at Lou; she is wiping away her tears and squeezing my hand so tightly my fingers have no circulation left.

'Lou, whatever happens, just keep your eyes closed when we go in the room, okay?'

She nods at me as we move closer. Henry and Ada are sitting opposite each other at the dining table. He glares at her as she cuts her meat.

'I'll be out this evening,' Henry states.

Ada glances up with half a smile. 'I have some news,' she whispers.

Henry raises his eyebrow. 'What news can you possibly have? You do nothing all day.'

Ada places her cutlery down on the plate and smiles. 'I'm pregnant. We are having a baby.'

'Well at least you have done something right. Teaching you manners does have its rewards,' Henry gloats.

Ada bows her head down. 'Yes, Henry,' she whispers.

Henry gets up from the table and struts towards her. Lowering his lips, he kisses the top of her head. 'We will throw a garden party to make the announcement, I think. Now go to your room, and I will see you when I get back.'

When he leaves, the maid walks in. She clears the table as Ada gets up.

'Is sir happy for you?' she asks.

'It's a terrible mess,' Ada says.

'As long as sir believes you, baby will have a better life.'

'It's just one big mess,' Ada cries.

My eyes widen as we step backwards out of the door. Now, the room changes back into the kitchen. Lou squeezes my hand, and I stare at her.

'What did all that mean?' Lou asks.

As I take in what Ada said to the maid, my eyes blink fast. I gasp, covering my mouth. Removing my palm so Lou can hear me, I reply, 'I think it means Ada's baby wasn't Henry's.'

'Huh? But they were married, weren't they?'

Rolling my eyes at Lou, I answer, 'I'm not explaining that now. We have to find Richard.'

Chapter 76

Richard stumbles in the darkness as Henry's eerie laugh echoes around them. The piercing screams jolt through Richard as he clasps his hands over his ears.

'Don't like the sound, Mr Harris?' Henry taunts.

Richard darts his eyes at Henry while crumbling to the ground. 'This is where you belong!' he states.

Henry bends down and, inches from Richard's face, his lips curl into a smirk. 'No, I don't belong here. However, my dear Mr Harris, you do.'

Returning to a standing position, Henry pulls at his jacket sleeves. Then with a glare back at Richard, Henry says, 'Now, if you had not interfered with my plans to use Ann to take my place, I being very gracious would have let you live out your death in my home but no more. It has been agreed for your betrayal that you, Mr Richard Harris, can take my place. And with you not around, I can deal with the old man and the girls very easily. Have fun, won't you!' Henry smirks.

'Go to hell,' Richard shouts.

A shrill screech sends shivers through Richard's body as he tries to block out the voices. Henry continues to glare at him while holding out his hand. 'The ring please.'

Richard stares at the cold, icy hand in front of him. The long pale palm outstretched with the thin fingers waiting to grab the ring. Richard slowly moves his eyes upwards to meet Henry's white blood-shot eyes.

'No!'

Henry's eyes widen as his nostrils flare. Cracking his knuckles, he seethes, 'What?'

'You heard me, Henry. I said no!'

'It's Mr Roberts to you.'

Richard shakes his head. 'Times have moved on; in case you were not aware. More to the point we are dead so you are no longer my master, Henry!' Richard snaps back.

Henry launches himself at Richard and grabs the scruff of his collar, 'Give me the damn ring.'

Richard stares into Henry's cold eyes. 'Why is the ring so important? Would it be because it can not only release you, but it can hold you here?'

Henry, baring his teeth, says, 'Ring now!'

Richard slides his hand into his pocket and pulls the ring out, holding it between his fingers as he stretches his arm out to the side. The diamonds and sapphires sparkle against the darkness and for a moment an eerie silence fills the air.

'Is this the ring?' Richard asks.

Henry's lip curl into a smile as he snatches the ring from Richard's hand. He holds it in front of his face and beams.

'Finally, I'm free,' Henry gloats.

Chapter 77

Henry disappears, leaving Richard alone. Stepping backwards, Richard's eyes dart back and forth but find no escape. The bleak surroundings of the darkness and images of suffering now come into focus. Opposite Richard, in an open room, a soul bolts for the doorway but a figure drags it back. A silvery blade cuts through the dark and the soul cries out as it plunges into its chest. Then the incident repeats with a piercing scream.

Running through the darkness, Richard stops.

'I am stuck between worlds. I'm neither dead nor alive, I'm just a ghost, so why can't I leave?' he shouts over the cacophony of screams.

A voice becomes audible. 'The poltergeist made a deal, and as long as he has the ring, you are stuck here.'

'The family of the house I reside in are in danger. I must be let out to help them,' Richard begs.

Nothing. He spins around and an empty room catches his eye. A dark figure with no face stands in the doorway. Staring at the figure, Richard's body trembles. He opens his mouth, but no words escape his lips as the figure steps forward.

'Are you the one who is taking Henry's place?' it asks.

Richard shakes his head as his eyes glaze over.

'Pity, as I don't like standing around. Get him back here.'

'I can't leave,' Richard stutters.

The figure stares at Richard. 'I know you are supposed to take his place, but why torture the innocent? Here, even the confident ones fall. They all pay, but Henry escapes and trades his evil soul for his victim. I will let you out, but you need to make a deal with me.'

Richard's eyes widen as his lips tremble. His muscles stiffen while his throat tightens. Richard grabs his neck as the figure's stare intensifies.

'Now you see what I can do. So, will you make a deal?'

Gasping for air, Richard forces himself to look at the figure. 'What are your terms?'

A sharp and icy trail runs over Richard neck and his breathing returns to normal. The figure disappears for a moment. A piece of paper appears in Richard's hand. He glances at the paper and words start to form across the page.

'I believe this is what you would call a contract,' the figure states.

Richard meets the figure's gaze for a moment before reading the terms.

'Those are my terms. Do you agree?'

Richard's hands tremble as the words sink in. He gulps a few times, sweat pouring down his face. He bolts his head upright. They stare at each other for a brief moment.

'Do you agree with the terms?' the figure asks once more.

'I do,' Richard says, as his trembling hand scribbles his signature across the page.

Chapter 78

Lou runs to the front door. She tugs on the handle and it opens. The rain lashes down and the wind howls through the trees. Squeezing Lou's hand, we step through the doorway, but when we get outside, the landscape changes and we are in a small room.

'What happened?' Lou asks.

Turning to face her, I see her lips start to quiver as her face goes pale.

'I'm not sure,' I answer. Out of the corner of my eye, I catch a glimpse of the staircase. 'Look—we are back in the house. If you look at the doorway, you can see the start of the staircase going down. Lou, I think we're in the attic.'

The sound of heated voices comes closer to the room. I pull Lou's arm and hide in the darkest corner of the room. Richard storms in, slamming the door behind him. Sweat is pouring down his face. His eyes are red, his lips trembling. Placing his head in his hands, his body jerks as he screams. The door shudders and Richard jumps. Turning to face the door, he steps back as it bursts open.

Henry struts inside. Tilting his head, he teases Richard. 'Do you miss her?'

'I want to see her. Please! Mr Roberts, I beg you.'

Henry smirks and lets out a laugh. 'Your plea is ignored, Mr Harris. My wife is dead because of you,' he snarls.

Shaking his head, Richard says, 'I saw you…'

'You saw me try to save my beloved wife, the mother of my son,' Henry snaps back. 'You drove her to suicide; she was happy before you came into our lives. If I never invited you to take the job then my beautiful Ada would still be alive.' Stepping closer to Richard, Henry grabs him by the throat and hisses, 'The only one to blame is you.'

Richard just stares at Henry, tears rolling down his face. 'Ada and I were happy. You made her life a misery.'

Henry rolls his eyes. The corners of his mouth turn downwards and then he spits in Richard's face. Lowering his chin, Henry glares at him.

'She took the vow to obey me. She also said in those vows she would be true, but she lied in church, and now she is dead because of you!'

Sniffling, Richard stares at Henry. Almost in a whisper, he says, 'I know what I saw. You killed her.'

'No, I did not. And if you are desperate to see her then may I suggest joining the whore?' Henry says as he lets go of Richard's throat.

Richard rubs his neck while he stares at Henry. Henry smiles at him as he straightens his jacket and struts towards the doorway. Turning back to Richard, a smirk creeps across his face.

'Her coffin was sealed this morning and she is now with the undertaker waiting for her final resting place. When you see her again, give her my best, won't you?'

Lou turns to me, her eyes wide. As she opens her mouth, the scenery changes once more. Now, Lou and I are back in the front doorway as Mum runs up the stairs and scoops us up in her arms.

Chapter 79

Lou continues to stare at me as Mum embraces us. Mum is moving her lips and Lou is responding but their words barely register in my mind. A pungent odour passes my nose, and I turn my head. Henry steps through the wall, grinning as he comes closer to Lou. He waves the ring as he basks in his glory. I nudge Lou with my elbow and nod at her while darting my eyes in his direction. She follows my gaze, and her face turns pale.

I jump and turn back to Mum as her eyes widen and she tilts her head.

'I'm sorry, Mum, but I was distracted,' I say.

'Are you okay?' Mum asks.

'Yes, but Henry is back and he has the ring,' I say, pointing to him.

Mum jumps up, pushing us behind her. Henry steps forward with a grin. Holding out his icy hand, he shows her the ring.

'Thank you for restoring it, and now it's back with its rightful owner,' Henry gloats.

His icy stare turns my stomach as blood continues to trickle down his cheek. He strolls forward and Mum pushes us back.

'Tut, tut, Lily. Pushing the girls back—what could I possibly do to them?' Henry asks.

Mum trembles the closer Henry gets. They stare at each other, and once he is standing in front of her, he leans in, baring his yellow teeth.

'What, no reply? Shame, as I do love our chats, however brief.'

Mum mumbles something, but he knocks her aside and grabs my arm. Turning back to Mum, he says, 'Your daughter and I have unfinished business.'

Mum turns pale, her eyes darting between us. Tears stream down her face while she holds out her hand for me to grab. I reach out, but she vanishes before my eyes.

'Let me go!' I scream, trying to free my hand from Henry's grip.

We appear in a graveyard and he tugs at my hand.

'Be grateful you are here and not the darkness!' he yells.

He drags me down a path, passing many headstones. A few have flowers but many are unkempt and unloved. The crisp leaves start to fall, and as we walk by, a breeze brushes my cheek. Henry stops in front of a headstone. Staring at the headstone, it reads:

In loving memory of
Ada Roberts

Tightening his grip, Henry starts to talk. 'So, my dear wife, I'm here to tell you that I have the ring in my possession. I gave this ring with love, and you betrayed me. This young girl is Ann, and she has volunteered to take my place.'

Turning my head, there is another headstone, which reads:

Here lies
Henry Roberts
Died 14th February 1947
Aged 60

Staring at the words, a smirk creeps across my face. *All he gets is "here lies".* The wind increases and blasts past me, knocking me off my feet. Dark clouds form around us and rain lashes down. Henry glares into the sky.

'I'm gaining my freedom, so get lost!' he yells.

A whisper in my ear is faint but becomes audible. 'You must get the ring.'

I squeeze my eyes shut. 'Who are you?' I cry.

'You must destroy the ring once you have it,' the voice insists.

'I can't.'

Henry thrusts me into the headstone, and the glisten of a blade appears from his pocket. A faint figure forms behind him. Henry, unaware, burns his stare into my eyes.

'Who were you talking too?' he demands.

I shrug my shoulders, and his eerie laugh echoes around me.

'No matter. You will be dead in a few minutes, and I will finally be free,' he snarls.

'Before you use the knife—I thought once you had the ring then you would be free?' I cry.

'I don't have to listen to you. Maybe you have got on my nerves and I just want to kill you!'

'You won't get away with this!' I shout.

'Say hello to Ada for me, won't you?' Henry seethes.

Chapter 80

The blade travels through air as the howling winds swallow my screams. The ring glistens, caught in a glimmer of light. Inches from my heart, Henry drops the knife and folds in two, gripping his stomach. Letting out a screech of pain, he falls to the floor, glaring at me as he tries to control his breathing. Baring his yellow teeth once more, blood pours from his mouth as he stumbles to his feet.

Grabbing the knife, he staggers towards me. I back away, raising my hands, and he quickens his pace. Clutching his chest, he grins at me.

'You are dying, so stay where you are and accept your fate.'

'No!' I cry.

As he gains on me, he stumbles and falls to the ground.

The voice whispers in my ear: 'Run and don't look back.'

I turn around and dash back up the path, but when I glance back at Henry, I trip and fall to the ground. Glancing down, I lift up my trouser leg and blood is seeping from a cut on my knee. I try and wipe the blood from my leg, but it continues to trickle down. A hand appears and grabs mine, pulling me to my feet.

'Come on, it's time to go,' the voice says.

My chest tightens and I shiver as I glance up at the person holding my arm. A slender old man with hints of brown in his hair is racing towards the exit, pulling on my arm. I try to free myself but he grips my hand tighter.

Henry bellows at me. 'Get back here, now!'

I turn to stare at Henry, who is struggling to get to his feet. My hand jerks and I gaze back at the man, tilting my head, raising my eyebrows.

'Hurry up before he catches us,' he says.

'Have we met before?' I ask.

'No, we have not.'

'Who are you, then?' I ask.

Turning to me, he answers, 'This is not the time or place. I know you are told not to trust strangers, but right now you have no choice, do you?'

Glancing over my shoulder, I see Henry gaining speed as he waves the knife. I turn back and break into a run.

'Ann, I'm gaining on you and your friend!' Henry shouts.

Pulling the man's hand, we are almost at the gate when an icy hand wraps around my neck, causing me to jolt backwards. Henry pushes the man forward, and he lets go of my hand. Stumbling to the floor, the man keeps his gaze on the ground.

'Did Art send you to rescue his niece?' Henry shouts.

The man continues to the face the floor, not uttering a word. His body shakes and he lets out a sigh.

'Answer me!' Henry demands. 'I know you can see and hear me.'

Chapter 81

My eyes dart from Henry to the man. A thrashing heartbeat echoes in my ears. I shake my head to free his grip, but Henry squeezes tighter.

'You are not getting free,' he snarls.

I claw my fingers against his icy hand while he laughs.

'Stop wriggling,' he demands.

Glaring at him, I clench my jaw as my nostrils flare. His grin widens the more I struggle.

'Carry on, and your death will be painful,' he hisses.

'Get off me!' I cry.

He releases my neck and I start to run, but he grabs my wrist, pulling me back. The man staggers to his feet, staring at the floor.

'Let her go,' he whispers.

Henry strolls towards the man, clenching his fist. 'Don't interfere. This is none of your business!'

The man shudders and steps back. 'She's just a girl,' he whispers.

Henry raises his hands and pushes him back. Stumbling backwards, the man regains his balance and takes a few more steps away.

'Haven't I seen you before?' Henry demands.

The man continues to stare at the floor.

'Look at me when I ask a question!' Henry screams. Nothing.

Henry barrels towards the man with his arms out but stops midway, falling to the ground, clenching his stomach. Glaring at him, I grit my teeth and kick him. I dart over to the man.

'Are you okay?' I ask.

He turns his head to me and a hint of a smile crosses his face.

'Let's get out of here,' he answers.

***

As the street comes into view, I turn to the man. 'Who are you?' I ask.

'I was just in the right place to help you,' he says. 'Now go home. Your family must be worried about you.'

I run down the pavement towards the house while the leaves fall around me. However, when I come to the house, the dark cloud still surrounds it and the rain lashes down. Entering the gate, I tiptoe up the stairs and push the door open. Stepping inside, a pungent smell hits my nose. The door slams shut, making me jump. I turn, but no one is there.

Turning the corner, Lou is in the kitchen doorway, crying. She rubs her eyes and runs towards me.

Henry's voice bellows, 'Finally, you are home! Come and join us in the kitchen.'

I enter the kitchen as Henry pokes Uncle Art in the chest.

'This is my house and I want you out. If you don't leave, you will suffer the consequences.'

Lou and I glance at each other and then back at them. Uncle Art bares his teeth and jabs Henry back.

'This is my home, and I will not be threatened out by a man who only gets his way by violence. So, if you are going to kill me, get it over with!' Uncle Art yells.

Henry clenches his hand and shoves Uncle Art. Lou is crying and tears roll down my face.

'You have what you want, leave my uncle alone!' Mum screams at Henry.

Henry turns to her and growls. Turning back to Uncle Art, he cracks his neck from side to side then lets out an eerie laugh.

'But do I, Lily? Do I?'

Chapter 82

Richard glides through the wall, entering the attic. Turning back, he sees the opening start to close but not before a voice whispers, 'Remember your deal.'

Trembling, he takes a gulp. 'I won't forget.'

Once the opening closes, Richard falls to his knees, burying his head in his hands.

'What have I done?' he yells.

A scream grabs his attention. Racing out of the room, the hallway is different. A woman is sobbing as she runs down the stairs. Richard frowns, scratching his cheek. His eyes dart back to the attic room, catching something. Edging back towards the attic, he overhears voices from the level below.

'Sir, sir,' a woman cries.

'What is it, Mary?'

'Mr 'arris. Please come,' she begs.

Richard pokes his head around the door. His furniture is in place. Glancing at the floor, a table is overturned, a shadow moving across it. Richard looks upwards, staggering back. His eyes widen as his jaw opens. Staring back at him is himself, swaying in mid-air, red-shot eyes bulging. A person passes through him, making Richard jolt.

'Mary, go and ring the police immediately.'

Mary nods, tears streaming down her face, and sniffles. The man turns, and Richard glares at him. Henry whisks out a handkerchief.

'Wipe your face, Mary—and for God's sake, stop crying. Now make the call,' he demands.

When she leaves, Henry turns back to the body and a smirk creeps across his face. 'Say hello to the whore for me, won't you?'

Richard launches himself at Henry, but he passes through him, falling to the floor. He jumps to his feet to turn around, but Henry is gone and so is the furniture.

Now, back in the present, a piercing cry draws him back. Shaking his head, Richard stays still and rubs his forehead. Why was he still seeing his death? What was missing? And why couldn't he remember it?

Another scream echoes around the house. Leaving the room, Richard follows the commotion. Getting closer, the stench of death becomes stronger. The rain lashes against the window as cracks of thunder strike. A bellowing laugh makes Richard tremble.

'Stop your sniffling!' Henry screams.

Richard tiptoes closer. He shudders when he is met with an eerie silence. Placing his hand on the doorframe, he jumps, when the silence is broken. *Brrrrr... brrrrr... brrrrr.* His eyes bulge, taking a step back.

Carefully, he edges forward. Taking a deep breath, he pokes his head around the corner.

Chapter 83

Lou picks up the phone. Henry bolts towards her, snatching the receiver from her hand. Grabbing her, he throws her across the room. A thud echoes as her head bounces against the wall. Her body goes limp, like a ragdoll, as she falls to the floor. Mum rushes towards her, scooping her up in her arms, while Henry replaces the handset.

'What did she ever do to you?' I scream.

Henry strolls over with a grin across his face. 'Welcome to hell,' he snarls.

I clench my fists, hitting him over and over, but he just stands there laughing.

'You really are pathetic, Ann,' Henry says.

'Lou, wake up!' Mum screams, hitting Lou's cheeks.

Tears roll down her face while she cradles Lou in her arms. Uncle Art opens his eyes and gazes over at Lou. His eyes glaze over and he swallows hard. He turns his head toward me and forces a smile for a moment. Then he looks up. Spinning around, I notice a figure in the doorway. Tilting my head, I step forward and catch Richard's eye. He points at me before hiding back in the shadows. I close my eyes before turning back around. Henry glares at me, tapping his foot on the floor.

'What were you doing?' he yells.

'Why should I tell you?' I snap.

'How dare you speak to me in that tone!'

'You hurt my sister!'

Henry bends down and closes the gap between us. Baring his teeth, he snarls, 'I will ask one more time and I expect an answer. What were you doing?'

Swallowing hard, I answer, 'I thought I saw something, but nothing is there.'

My body trembles as we continue to stare at each other. My pulse races and I clench my jaw. The room plunges into darkness as a crackle of lightning strikes. I shoot over to Mum and kneel beside her.

'Is Lou alright?' I ask.

Shaking her, Mum wraps her arm around me, pulling me in close. 'She is breathing but she hasn't opened her eyes yet,' she whispers.

I glance at Lou in Mum's arms. She looks so peaceful. When I look up, writing starts to appear across the wall in bold red.

Don't let him win. Get the ring back.

'Who are you?' I scream.

Mum's eyes dart to me. Henry races over. 'Who are you talking to?'

With a shaking hand, I point to the wall. He turns to look at it and then back at me.

'I don't know what you are playing at, but it won't work,' he says.

When he walks off toward Uncle Art, who is still lying on the floor, I glance back to the wall. More writing appears.

Don't tell him. You must hurry before history repeats itself.

Chapter 84

Dragging Uncle Art to his feet by his shirt, Henry yells, 'It's now time, Art, for you to meet death, and for me to have my second chance!'

Getting to my feet, I snap at Henry. 'First you want me to take your place, then Lou and now Uncle Art. Can't you make up your mind?'

'Ann, what are you doing? Sit back down,' Mum cries, pulling on my arm.

Henry glares at me once more. His nostrils flare and his eyes widen while his transparent chest moves in and out. 'Listen to your mother,' he demands.

'Do as your mum says!' Uncle Art interjects.

Shrugging my arm free, I step closer to Henry. Narrowing my eyes, I take another step. 'I won't listen. Leave my Uncle Art alone, and I want my mum's ring back!' I shout, holding out my hand.

The voice whispers in my ear. 'He put it in his pocket. And yes, I'm the one who wrote the messages on the wall. Many people are relying on you. You can do this.'

Who is relying on me? There are so many questions going around in my head. My body trembles and my hand starts to shake. I back away as my pulse races. Muttering under my breath, I ask, 'Where's Richard?'

'He is here, but you have to do this,' the whisper responds.

Stumbling backwards, I reply, 'I can't; he's scary.'

'Yes, you can. Now go.'

I edge forward. Sweat drips down my face. I close my eyes, but when I open them, Henry is still standing over Uncle Art. Henry kicks him.

'Come on, old man; time to meet death,' he says, ignoring my request.

Taking a deep breath, I yell, 'Henry, I asked for the ring. Now give it back!'

Henry lets out a sigh and turns back to me. 'You really are getting on my nerves. The ring is mine.'

'You gave it away as a gift. You can't take back something you gave away. Uncle Art found the ring, so it rightfully belongs to him. And Uncle Art chose to give it to my mum, so it is hers.'

Henry smirks and takes the ring from his pocket. He stretches out his arm and opens his hand. 'Take it from my icy hand, if you dare. If you can grab it then you can keep it,' he taunts.

I look quickly around the room. Mum's eyes widen with fear and Uncle Art is shaking his head. I tiptoe closer as my hand trembles.

'I'm waiting, Ann.'

'I will get it, Henry!'

'You are very sure of yourself for a young girl. Personally, I think you are stupid and cocky.'

As I take another step, Henry shakes his head. 'Hurry up—I don't have all day,' he growls.

I extend my arm and open my hand.

'Almost there, Ann. Take it. I dare you,' he baits me.

Shuffling forward, I stretch my arm out further. The ring glistens in his pale, icy hand, begging me to take it. Inches away, and the sweat is now pouring down my face. The gap between the ring and my fingers is closing. I step closer, and as my fingers touch the ring, Henry closes his hand, but I pull my hand away just in time.

Chapter 85

Keeping my hand shut tight, I glare at Henry for a moment. Turning on my heels, I sprint from the room and up the stairs. I use a sliver of light through the hall window as my guide.

The voice whispers in my ear. 'Don't stop. Keep going. You can do this.'

I stop for a moment at the bottom of the attic stairs. Glancing into the darkness, I take a deep breath, closing my eyes. When I open them, I place my foot on the first step. My racing pulse stops me going any further, getting louder in my ears.

Richard appears and smiles. 'You don't have much time. Now go!' he says.

'I need to tell you something, Richard—' I say, but he cuts me off.

'Ann, there is no time. Go, and keep your hand closed until you get there.'

'But it's scary up there; I can't—'

Richard interrupts me again. 'You can do this, and you will be fine. I promise.' He places his pale hand over mine and widens his smile. 'Go!'

My eyes dart from him to the darkness leading to the attic. I cover my face, but he pulls my hand away and pushes me up the stairs. My body trembles with each step. As I turn the corner, Henry's voice bellows throughout the house.

'Give me back my ring, Ann!'

Shaking, I bolt up the stairs, and after an eerie silence, Henry bellows again.

'Don't ignore me, Ann!'

My mum screams, 'Ann, hide! He's coming after you.'

I enter the room and the moon shines through the window. The stars twinkle, highlighting Ada's picture. Rushing over to the window, I glance around the room but it's empty. I start to hyperventilate. The ring is in my hand, but there is nothing to damage it with. I start blubbering as my eyes dart around the room.

Glancing out into the pitch-black hallway, I see something come into the light. A hammer is making its way towards me in mid-air. I jump as it gets closer. Sliding along the wall, the hammer drops to the floor in front of me. I wait for a moment but nothing happens. I pick up the hammer, keeping my eyes on the door.

A bolt of lightning strikes and the room grows cold. Henry is getting closer now. He knows I took the ring. My stomach churns and the hammer shakes in my hand.

'I will let you live if you give me the ring right now,' Henry demands, getting closer. His footsteps stomp up the last few stairs. My eyes widen as I wait for him to appear.

'I'm getting closer, Ann. Give me what I want, and no harm will come to you.'

'You always say that,' I cry.

The stench of rotting flesh is getting stronger. His eerie laugh echoes around the room. His cold fingers appear around the doorframe. I glide against the smooth wall, away from the door, when his white eyes pouring with blood appear out of the darkness. He bares his teeth as he strolls into the room.

Holding out his hand, he says, 'The ring, please.'

Chapter 86

I stay still and glare at him, keeping my hand shut tight. He wanders towards me with a grin.

'Give me the ring and I will not harm you,' he says in a calming tone.

I knock my arm against the other wall, and when I glance back at Henry, he is walking towards me as he lets out his eerie laugh.

'This room is so important to me. Ah, the memories.' Henry beams.

He is only a few steps away when he disappears. It is now daylight; the sun is streaming through the window and the room is furnished with the basics. Richard is pushing a table towards me close to the window. He glances at the sun and sniffles. Climbing onto the table, he puts a hook into the ceiling and ties a rope to it. His clothes are dishevelled and dirty. His dark hair is all over the place and his shirt is unbuttoned. He picks up the picture of Ada from his bed and starts sobbing.

He keeps repeating the same words over and over: 'I'm so sorry.'

His hand trembles as he picks up a glass. He downs its contents and shudders. He walks up to the table and steps onto it. Holding the rope in his hand, he glances back to the picture. Turning back to the rope, he says, 'Oh God, what am I doing? Ada would be so disappointed in me.'

Jumping off the table, he takes the picture back in his hand. 'I love you and I want to be with you, my darling, but I know you would want me to keep an eye on your son, in case Henry is cruel to him.'

Henry appears in the doorway with his arms folded, glaring at Richard. 'I will never be cruel to my son, Henry. At least we can thank the lord she never gave birth to your child,' he snarls.

As Henry steps into the room, Richard adds, 'Don't know if you knew, but Ada was pregnant when she died and it was yours. At least the world doesn't have another one of you.'

Richard flies at Henry and knocks him to the ground. Sitting on top of Henry, Richard throws a few punches, but each time, Henry just laughs, saying, 'Is that all you have?'

Henry pushes Richard off, and he falls to the floor. Henry crawls toward him and punches him in the stomach. Richard flinches, but before he can react, Henry sits on his chest and places his hands around his throat. Richard tries to peel his fingers from his neck, but Henry squeezes harder. Richard kicks his legs, still trying to get free, but after a few minutes, his eyes close. Henry gets off and sits next to him. He pulls a cigar from his pocket, lights it and starts humming.

Richard lets out a slight cough. I gasp and a smile creeps across my face.

'You are okay,' I cry, although neither of them can hear me.

I continue to observe the memory.

Henry glares at Richard, letting out a growl when he notices the rope. His lips curl up into a smile. 'So, you were going to do the decent thing after all and hang yourself. Well, we wouldn't want to keep Ada waiting, now would we?'

'No!' I scream. My vision blurs as teardrops roll down my face; each tastes salty as they enter my mouth.

My eyes widen as I stare at Henry getting to his feet. He drags a limp Richard over to the table. Slumping him over it, Henry then climbs up. Undoing the rope, he places the noose around Richard's neck. Throwing the rope back over the hook, Henry then proceeds to pull Richard up. As Richard awakes to find himself hanging, he tries to free himself. Looking down at Henry, he begs, 'Please let me down; you don't have to do this.'

'No. Besides, the police believe you killed my wife, and they will take this as a sign of a guilty conscience. Any last requests?'

'Please, let me live.'

'Nope,' Henry gloats, kicking the table out from underneath Richard.

Now, I'm back facing the poltergeist Henry with his eyes glaring at me.

'The ring!' he barks.

Chapter 87

Another bolt of lightning strikes near to us, and Henry growls in its direction, 'Go away. You lost and I won.'

Shuffling away, I get to the other side of the room. Screaming at him, I yell, 'I know what you did!'

Henry stops and stares at me, narrowing his eyes. 'How did you get there? No matter, I'm coming to get the ring.'

I open my hand, and the ring glistens in the moonlight. A smile creeps across my face, and I let it go. It rolls in the air as it gets closer to the floor. Henry starts to move, but I hold out the hammer. He stops. The ring clinks against the wood floor. Henry puts out his hand, waving it at me, and takes a step back.

'Ann, lets discuss this,' he says.

I ignore his plea and raise the hammer above my head. I slam it downwards, keeping my eye on Henry. He lets out a laugh, and when I glance at the ring, it's still whole.

'Oh my. You really are a bad shot, aren't you? Definitely a girl,' Henry taunts.

I let out a screech as I swing the hammer through the air. Keeping my eyes on the ring and not Henry, I hit it. The ring bounces to the side. Henry lets out a scream while clutching his stomach. *Oh, this is fun.*

'Take this!' I boast as the hammer hits the ring again. A sapphire stone breaks loose, and Henry crumbles to the floor.

Holding out his arm, Henry whispers, 'Please stop! Show mercy.'

'Umm, let me think… No. You hurt my uncle, my mum and my sister and showed no mercy to them.'

Another hit of the hammer, and the darkness starts to clear. The blood on the walls starts to fade. Henry glares at me.

'I should have killed you in the darkness,' he snarls.

I keep smashing the ring until it is flat. The sapphires and diamonds lie strewn across the floor. I wander over to Henry as he lies in a foetal position.

'You killed Ada and Richard and your—' I yell, when Richard stops me. 'You need to go now, Ann.'

'But… but…'

'I know, but this part is not for the living to see. Especially a child,' Richard insists.

I leave the room and Henry yells after me, 'One day, Ann, I will find a way back, and when I do, I will find you.'

My eyes widen, but Richard closes the door.

Chapter 88

Henry, still lying on the floor, glares at Richard as he strolls to the window. Henry tries to pull himself up but collapses. Gasping for air, he manages to say, 'Aren't you going to say something?'

Turning around, Richard stares at Henry, folding his arms. 'The only thing I want to know is what did Ann mean, "you killed Ada and Richard"?'

Henry lets out a weak laugh and grins at him. 'My dear Richard, don't you remember?'

Darting towards Henry, Richard kneels beside him and grabs his hair, pulling his head back. Henry, still laughing, jokes, 'I've never seen this side of you. I think I'm starting to like you even more.'

'Cut the crap and answer the question with a straight answer,' Richard snarls.

'All these years, you thought you had committed suicide, but the secret is I murdered you. You were pining over my late wife. Sad, really.'

'Get to the point, Henry.'

'I watched you from the doorway and you were ready to hang yourself. However, it seems you had a change of heart. Something about keeping an eye out for my son, Henry. He is a truly ungrateful child,' Henry says, coughing while he tries to sit up. 'I gave him the best schools, money, and do you know what he did? After his twenty-fifth birthday, he ignored me. Probably didn't even come to my funeral. Although, when I visited Ada's grave, a man placed flowers at her grave—can you believe that? And my headstone is rotting away.'

Richard raises his eyebrows while shaking his head. 'Are you really surprised, Henry? I'm sure the boy had his reasons, like he saw the real you. Now get to the point and stop digressing!'

'Where was I? Oh yes, change of heart and Henry. Anyway, I came in and we started fighting. I started to strangle you, and when you closed your eyes, I stopped. Enjoying my moment with a smoke, you coughed. I spotted the noose and managed to get you up there. Then—and this is the delightful part—you came around while dangling there, pleading to be let down, but the good person that I am, I kicked the table away and delighted in your suffering. And do you want to know the best part? Mary the maid found your body and came and got me, which gave me my alibi.'

Richard's eyes widen. He opens his mouth, but no words come out as they glare at each other. Richard rubs his neck as he steps back. 'Why… Why?'

'My wife was obedient before you came along, and knew her place. Do you know I heard her say she was going to leave me?'

'You didn't care about her and you never loved her, but I did.'

'So what, you loved her—'

'I still love her, you bastard! But you never loved her.'

'What has love got to do with it? We were married. It was her duty to accept her lot and be happy.'

'How many other women were there?' Richard demands.

'You were my butler; you made the arrangements… but Laura and Emma. Now they were fun,' Henry says with a grin.

'Exactly my point. You could have found happiness with a woman who loved you and you her. So why hold on to Ada?'

'Her family had money and she was easy to mould, until you came to my house. Are we done?' Henry snarls.

Richard clenches and unclenches his fists, grinding his teeth. 'I have one last question, Henry. Did you kill your father, John?'

Henry rolls his eyes. 'That bastard wouldn't sign the house over to me. He told me to stop taking his money and get a job. So, yes, I killed him. He'd called me over one evening in September 1910—you always remember the date of your first kill. Anyway, he fell asleep after giving me a lecture. I took a pillow and smothered him to death. I needed the money; I had debts and a fiancée.'

Richard's eyes bulge at Henry, his nostrils flaring as his body shakes.

Henry grins. 'You want to hit me; I can see it. If I were you, I would. But you are hesitating. The question is why?'

Richard folds his arms as his lips curl into a smile. 'An old friend has come to see you.'

Chapter 89

Narrowing his eyes at Richard, Henry lets out an eerie laugh. 'Who could you possibly know that would want to see me?'

A slit in the wall opens to the darkness. Henry scoffs, 'Is that it? Some kind of portal?'

Richard grins at Henry. 'Oh, but Henry, it is the darkness, and while you made arrangements for anyone but you to serve your time... Well, I made a deal of my own.' Kneeling back down beside Henry, Richard smiles. 'I'll admit, if it wasn't for Ann, I would have to spend eternity suffering because of you, but Ann came through. And, well... your torturer is here to take you home.'

The faceless figure enters the attic room, hovering in front of the darkness. The pungent stench of death floats in the air as gurgling screams echo from the darkness. Richard brings his sleeve to his nose and steps back. Henry crawls along the floor, away from the figure, as his eyes widen and his body starts to shake.

The figure whispers through the air, 'Henry Roberts, we meet once more.'

Turning to face the figure, Henry's eyes almost burst from their sockets. 'Stay away from me. I got away from you, and I'm not going back.'

The figure steps closer. 'Henry, I have a new home for you. One that you can never escape.'

Crawling away, Henry hits the wall. Leaning against it, his breathing becomes shallow and he starts to hyperventilate. 'The things you did... never!'

'Henry, thanks to Richard here, we have your full confession. And because of your erratic behaviour as a poltergeist, your memories leaked and you showed the girls death and murder and violence.'

'So?' Henry whispers.

Moving forward, the figure adds, 'We now have a complete picture and have adjusted the charges against you, and your punishment—'

'Is it time served?' Henry enquires. 'Can I be with my beloved wife, Ada, who I miss dearly?' he asks with a smile as sweat pours from his brow.

'Henry, you are lying. You never loved your wife and will never be permitted to reunite with her. You murdered her in cold blood and did the same to Richard, passing both incidents as suicides. You escaped human justice, but never will you escape justice in the afterlife. Now you have to come with me.'

The figure walks over to Henry. Shaking his head, he keeps repeating, 'No... no... no...'

The figure raises its icy arm and Henry lets out a screech. Richard steps back into the corner of the room as the figure moves its arm. Henry floats up the wall and then his body dashes across the room, hitting the wall on the other side. The cracking of bones makes Richard flinch as Henry lets out a shrill scream.

'Stop it! I have done nothing wrong!' Henry begs.

The figure draws him towards itself. 'Denial will not stop the punishment. I, like many others, was created to punish people like you. This is just a warm up, Henry. As you know, I can't do my best work until we are alone.'

Henry gulps, his lips trembling.

'Stay put, won't you? There's a good boy,' the figure says.

Large clamps appear around Henry's wrists and feet as he hangs in mid-air. He struggles to free himself.

The figure turns to Richard and says, 'Thank you for your help in returning Henry Roberts. Sadly, you cannot be free from this house—'

'But you said—'

'I know what we agreed, but in light of his threat to the child, it has been decided that until the girls die a natural death, you are now their protector. Upon the last one's death, you may then be allowed to rest. May I also suggest you listen to what Ann was about to say.'

'What about Ada? Can I see her?' Richard begs.

'No. Once the last one has passed away, only then can you ask that question.'

Facing Henry once more, the figure heads towards the darkness, dragging Henry by the hair.

'Mr Harris, I will find a way—believe me, I will—and I promise you, I will kill the girls and you!' Henry shouts, struggling to get free.

Once through the portal, it seals behind him.

Chapter 90

After Mum gets Uncle Art to his chair, he keeps pointing to his throat. Mum looks at me and says, 'Ann, get Uncle Art some water, please.'

Nodding in agreement, I run to the kitchen. Grabbing a clean glass, I turn on the tap until it's cold and fill it. Turning around, a girl is smiling at me. I open my mouth, but no words come out.

She steps forward and says, 'Hi. Sorry if I scared you. The writing on the wall was the only thing I could think of.'

My eyes widen. I sway slightly, having to put the glass down. 'I thought…' I stutter. 'Ada… I thought it was Ada,' I manage to say.

'Who? Look, I just came here to thank you. The poltergeist murdered me and my friends when we brought him back.'

'You brought him back? Why?'

'At the time, it was something fun. We never thought chanting with a ring in our hands would really work.'

'Well, it did. My uncle is badly hurt and my sister is still sleeping after being hurt,' I snap.

'I'm really sorry, but thank you for rescuing us and getting rid of him.'

Sighing, I let out a breath. 'I just wanted him to leave us alone.'

'Thank you,' she says before disappearing.

Grabbing the glass, I head back to the living room. Richard is sitting on the sofa with his head in his hands.

I hand the glass to Uncle Art and say, 'Are you alright, Richard?'

He lifts his head to meet my gaze and says, 'I am glad it is over and you are alright.'

'Lou hasn't opened her eyes yet,' Mum interjects.

Richard looks towards Lou and smiles. 'She will be fine. Just call the doctor to make sure.'

'The doctor is on his way,' Mum replies.

Uncle Art sips his water and stares at Richard. 'But you don't get your happy ending, do you?' he asks.

Richard shakes his head and glances at the floor. 'No, I don't,' he whispers. Richard lifts his head and gazes at me. 'What were you trying to tell me earlier?'

'I saw a memory; I think it was Ada's. She said that the baby Henry was really yours,' I answer.

Richard's eyes widen as he gets to his feet and blurts out, 'What?!'

My mouth opens, but a knock at the door distracts me. I dart for the door and find a letter, which reads: 'Give to the ghost, Richard. When read, I'll be outside, waiting.'

I return to the living room with the letter and hand it to Richard. He steps back and keeps turning it around in his hand. Impatient, I yell, 'Open it!'

'Ann!' Uncle Art shouts.

'Sorry,' I say, and turn back to Richard. 'Please open the letter. It might be good news.'

Richard frowns at me as he opens the letter. His eyes dart across the page, and his hand trembles as he keeps reading.

'What does it say?' I ask.

Richard glances up at me and then to Uncle Art and Mum as he reads out the letter.

My darling son Henry,
When you read this letter, I will be long gone. You have a right to the truth, and I am so sorry I wasn't able

to tell you in person. As a young woman, I met a man, and if you believe in such things, I fell in love instantly.

However, your grandmother scared him off, and so I married Henry, planning to never see that man again. A few years into the marriage, he walked back into my life and all the feelings came back. I tried to ignore them, but every time I looked at him, the feelings only got stronger. So, we started seeing each other. I'm not proud of what I did, and I should be telling you how sorry I am, but I'm not, because I loved Richard.

The only barrier in our way was our class. You see, Richard was our butler. I wanted to start a new life, but I was terrified of what people would say if I did. This meant I stayed in an unhappy marriage. The level of cruelty and violence that Henry forced upon me was unbearable, but Richard's love got me through each day.

The reason I am explaining this to you is because Henry is not your natural father. During my time with Richard, I fell pregnant. Henry had been away on business, and this is how I know Richard Harris is your natural father. The only regret I have is that we were never a family and I never got to tell Richard I was expecting you, our son, as he would have been so happy. He is a good man, and I really hope you get to know each other and get on well. I am truly sorry you had to find out by letter. Please know that I love you both, and I am very proud of you.

All my love
Your mother.

No one speaks for a moment. When Richard leaves the room, I dart for the door, but Uncle Art raises his voice, 'Ann, leave Richard alone.'

'But I want to see how this ends.'

Uncle Art raises his eyebrows at me, and I step back into the room. Wandering to the sofa where Lou is lying asleep, I fall onto the cushion, and the dust particles float in the air. There are audible voices behind me, so I turn around, resting my chest against the back of the sofa. Putting my arms on the back cushions, I lean into the window and see Richard embracing a man outside.

'Ann, sit back down,' Uncle Art shouts.

'Richard is hugging a man,' I reply, turning to Uncle Art. 'It's the man who rescued me from the graveyard and from Henry. Your milkman, Rich, is with them.'

'Oh, let me have a look,' Mum says, rushing to the window.

'Lily!'

'Uncle Art, don't you want to see this?' Mum asks.

Uncle Art rolls his eyes, shaking his head. 'I think they might come in shortly, because not everyone can see ghosts. Now come away from the window!'

Mum sits back down in the chair. 'Who are they?' she asks.

'I'm guessing the older man would be Richard's son, and Rich, the milkman, would be his grandson. But you can ask when they come inside.'

I slide back into the sofa, when Lou stirs.

Mum cries out, 'Louise, you're alright!'

'Am I in trouble?' she asks as pushes herself up.

'No, why?'

'You only call me Louise when I've done something wrong.'

Staring at each other, we smile. I scoot over and pull her into a hug. Lou pulls away and glares at me. 'What are you doing?' she asks.

'I'm giving you a hug, because you're okay.'

'Well, I'm fine, so get off me. It doesn't mean I like you.'

I nudge her with my elbow and she does the same. 'Same here, Lou. Same here.'

Author Profile

 I wrote as a hobby for many years, but suddenly, I lost my way. I decided to take up a free writing course at The Open University and loved it so much that I started a degree in English and Creative Writing. At the same time, I wrote my first book, dealing with a phobia I have, and found it to be therapeutic, but more importantly I discovered that I really love to write!

I am now studying for my Master's Degree in Forensic Psychology alongside developing a small but a sustainable business tutoring English and exam skills, which provides me with the time to write, learn and educate. I have rediscovered a passion for the written word and have become an advocate for the importance of reading with all my students.

Twitter: @cathblackmore
Facebook: @cathblackmore19
Website: www.catherineblackmore.com

***

What Did You Think of *Mr Roberts' House*?

A big thank you for purchasing this book. It means a lot that you chose this book specifically from such a wide range on offer. I do hope you enjoyed it.

Book reviews are incredibly important for an author. All feedback helps them improve their writing for future projects and for developing this edition. If you are able to spare a few minutes to post a review on Amazon then, from the bottom of my heart, thank you very much.

Publisher Information

Rowanvale Books provides publishing services to independent authors, writers and poets all over the globe. We deliver a personal, honest and efficient service that allows authors to see their work published, while remaining in control of the process and retaining their creativity. By making publishing services available to authors in a cost-effective and ethical way, we at Rowanvale Books hope to ensure that the local, national and international community benefits from a steady stream of good quality literature.

For more information about us, our authors or our publications, please get in touch.

www.rowanvalebooks.com
info@rowanvalebooks.com